Praise for Richard T. Ryan'

The Vatican Cameos

Winner of the Underground Book Reviews' "Novel of the Year" Award.

Winner Silver Medal in the Readers' Favorite book-award contest.

"[*The Vatican Cameos* is] an extravagantly imagined and beautifully written Holmes story." – Lee Child, NY Times Bestselling author and the creator of Jack Reacher

"Once you've read *The Vatican Cameos*, you'll find yourself eagerly awaiting the next in Ryan's series." – Fran Wood, What Fran's Reading for nj.com

"Richard T. Ryan's *The Vatican Cameos* is an excellent pastiche-length novel, very much in the spirit of the original Holmes stories by Sir Arthur Conan Doyle." – Dan Andriacco, author of a host of Holmes' tales as well as the blog, bakerstreetbest.com

"Loved it! A must read for all fans of Sherlock Holmes!" – Caroline Vincent, Bits about Books

"Richard Ryan channels Dan Brown as well as Conan Doyle in this successful novel." – Tom Turley, Sherlockian author

"If you enjoy deeply researched historical fiction, combined with not one but two mystery/thriller stories, then you will really enjoy this excellent Sherlock Holmes pastiche." – Craig Copland, author of New Sherlock Holmes Mysteries

"A great addition to the Holmes Canon. Definitely worth a read." – Rob Hart, author of *The Warehouse* and the Ash McKenna series

"*The Vatican Cameos* opens with a familiar feel for fans of Arthur Conan Doyle's original Sherlock Holmes stories. The plotting is clever, and the alternating stories well-told." – Crime Thriller Hound

"A masterful spin on the ageless Sherlock Holmes. Somewhere I'm certain Sir Arthur Conan Doyle himself is standing and cheering." – Jake Needham, author of the Jack Sheperd and Inspector Samuel Tay series

The Stone of Destiny

"Sometimes a book comes along that absolutely restores your faith in reading. Such is the 'found manuscript' of Dr. Watson, *The Stone of Destiny*. Exhilarating, superb narrative and a cast of characters that are as dark as they are vivid. ... A thriller of the very first rank." – Ken Bruen, author of *The Guards, The Magdalen Martyrs,* and many other novels, as well as the creator of the Jack Taylor series

"A wonderful read for both the casual Sherlock Holmes fan and the most die-hard devotees of the beloved character." – Terrence McCauley, author of *A Conspiracy of Ravens* and *A Murder of Crows*

"Somewhere Sir Arthur Conan Doyle is smiling. Ryan's *The Stone of Destiny* is a fine addition to the Canon." – Reed Farrel Coleman, NY Times Bestselling author of *What You Break*

"Full of interesting facts, the story satisfies and may even have you believing that Holmes and Watson actually existed." – Crime Thriller Hound

"Ryan's Holmes is the real deal in [*The Stone of Destiny*]. One hopes the author is hard at work on the next adventure in this wonderfully imagined and executed series." – Fran Wood, What Fran's Reading for nj.com

"Mystery lovers will enjoy reading *The Stone of Destiny: A Sherlock Holmes Adventure* by Richard T. Ryan." – Michelle Stanley, Readers' Choice Awards

The Druid of Death

"The clever solution, which echoes one from a golden age classic, is the book's best feature." – Publishers Weekly

"*The Druid of Death* is clever and fun, a winning combination. The setting — Victorian England — and the Druidic lore are absolutely captivating. This is my favorite kind of mystery." – Criminal Element

" ... the Druidic detail and the depiction of 19th-century London are fascinating and delightful." – Kirkus Reviews

"Where many of the tangent series have been challenged to keep these characters [Holmes and Watson] fresh, this author has accomplished not only that but made them enjoyable too." – Jennie Reads

"Ryan creates a thoroughly enjoyable pastiche, giving readers just what you'd expect from such a mystery. The suspense is tangible, and the detection methodologies quirky. He's right on the money with his characterizations of all the usual players, especially Holmes and Watson." – Barbara Searles @thebibliophage.com

"A stunning achievement!" – Ken Bruen, author of *The Guards* and creator of Jack Taylor

"*The Druid of Death*? Sign me up! Sherlock Holmes and Dr. Watson find themselves caught up in a diabolical game of cat-and-mouse as the body count starts to rise. I devoured this book in an evening; you will too." – Leah Guinn, The Well-Read Sherlockian blog

The Merchant of Menace

Short-listed for the annual Drunken Druid Award.

"Oh, what a joy it is to meet Sherlock Holmes and Dr. Watson again! *The Merchant of Menace* is an exciting adventure of priceless valuables, great detective work and just the kind of devilish adversary we love to read about." – Mattias Boström, author of *From Holmes to Sherlock: The Story of the Men and Women Who Created an Icon*

"This rousing, intriguing, devilishly fun caper, well-executed and well-paced, had me hooked from the first page. The dutiful Watson, Holmes' deductive skills, and a worthy nemesis to rival the evil Moriarty himself, make this cat-and-mouse adventure a page-turning, edge-of-your-seat coaster ride well worth taking." – Tracy Clark, author of *Broken Places* and *Borrowed Time* and the creator of Cass Raines

"[*The Merchant of Menace* is] an absolute humdinger of a novel …It is beautifully written, erudite and hugely entertaining." – Ken Bruen, the author of *The Ghosts of Galway* and the creator of Jack Taylor

"The wonderfully titled *The Merchant of Menace* has all the familiarity of a lost Holmesian tale. An enjoyable adventure from the ever reliable Richard T. Ryan." – The Crime Thriller Hound

"Ryan has a real flair for capturing the language of Holmes and Watson, their foibles, and the dynamics of their relationship. He has created an antagonist and series of crimes that Conan Doyle would have been proud of." – Caramerrollovesbooks blog

"...[Holmes] encounters a rather delicious new 'villain'; this one can give Moriarty a run for his money but instead of trying to one-up the brilliance of Doyle's Moriarty, Ryan pays homage in the making of his *Merchant*." – The Caffeinated Reader

"With an intriguing premise and a cunning plot, *The Merchant of Menace* will delight Sherlockians of all stripes. Richard T. Ryan has given us a gripping mystery and a loving tribute to the Great Detective." – Daniel Stashower, author of *Teller of Tales: The Life of Arthur Conan Doyle*

Through a Glass Starkly

"Deftly blending Conan Doyle and Dan Brown, Richard Ryan's *Through a Glass Starkly* offers an intriguing mix of history and mystery. Remaining true to the Canon in his depictions of the iconic Holmes and Watson, Ryan also delivers a mystery that should satisfy even the most demanding Sherlockian." – Robert Dugoni, NY Times Bestselling author of *The Eighth Sister* and the creator of Tracy Crosswhite

"Ryan's Watsonian voice is superb, and as with his earlier novels the author has included several affectionate nods to the characters, stories, and intrigues of the original Canon. These twists and turns make this an engrossing and enjoyable read, as do the variety of colourful locations chosen for the action. From a secret *pied-a-terre* in Paris, to the Whispering Gallery in St. Paul's Cathedral, we are carried along at a frenetic pace. I previously read, and thoroughly enjoyed, *The Druid of Death. Through a Glass Starkly* is even better!" – Sherlock Holmes Society of London

"Mr. Ryan masterfully creates a totally engrossing and suspenseful adventure of international intrigue, kidnapping and murder." – Wendy Heyman Marshaw, author, *Mrs. Hudson's Kitchen*

"Another brilliant addition to the Sherlock Holmes Canon." – Bruce Robert Coffin, author of the Detective Byron mysteries

"Slap on your deerstalker and grab a pipe, Richard Ryan's Sherlock Holmes strikes again. With head-scratching twists and puzzling turns, even Arthur Conan Doyle would be hard-pressed to solve this mystery. *Through a Glass Starkly* will satisfy even the most ardent Holmes fans." – Jean M. Roberts @thebookdelight,com and the author of *The Heron*

"Richard T. Ryan does it again with *Through a Glass Starkly*. His latest pastiche featuring Sir Arthur Conan Doyle's legendary team of Holmes and Watson. It is an engrossing, twisty, delicious adventure involving a missing, priceless codex, Europe on the verge of war, a mysterious woman, and shadowy figures roaming the London docks. Great fun! – Tracy Clark, author of the Cass Raines Chicago mystery series

Three May Keep a Secret

"Richard T. Ryan's *Three May Keep a Secret* [is] a pitch-perfect adventure that pits Conan Doyle's great detective against a master criminal…It's a tale of fabulous jewels, brilliant forgeries, cunning disguises and a Watson double-act that will make every writer who's ever penned a Holmes pastiche green with 'Why didn't I think of that?'" – Jeffrey Hatcher, screenwriter for *Mr. Holmes*

"Richard Ryan has yet again given us one of his well-crafted yet exciting and entertaining novels of Sherlock Holmes. Settle in for several hours of fun reading." – Robert Katz, MD, BSI

"… the book's strengths, including the imaginative setup, make Ryan's taking up Conan Doyle's mantle again welcome. Fans of traditional pastiches will enjoy this." – Publishers Weekly

"The tour de force in the book is the presence of a criminal mastermind, a worthy replacement for Professor Moriarty, whose shadows are broodingly present in the adventure." – *Sherlock Holmes Society of India*

"Oh man, this was an intense cat-and-mouse game and I loved it! It was really well-written and well-researched …I loved the banter between Holmes and Watson, and as always I liked how every little thing that Holmes does has a purpose. And of course his exceptional deduction skills are always on point!" – thereadingowlvina (Elvina Ulrich)

The Poisoned Pawn:

A Sherlock Holmes Adventure

By Richard T, Ryan

Hardcover ISBN 978-1-80424-084-7
Paperback ISBN 978-1-80424-085-4
AUK ePub 978-1-80424-086-1
AUK PDF 978-1-80424-087-8

Published by MX Publishing
335 Princess Park Manor, Royal Drive, London, N11 3GX
www.mxpublishing.co.uk

Cover design by Brian Belanger

Once again, this book is dedicated to my wife, Grace,
whose patience with me could put Job to shame.

It's also dedicated to my mother who instilled in me a
love of reading
and my father who encouraged me in all my endeavors.
I miss them both terribly.

Introduction

The Poisoned Pawn is the seventh Sherlock Holmes novel to make its way from the tin dispatch box, which I won at an estate auction in Scotland, to print.

In the first six previously published books, it seems obvious that Holmes was the driving force behind several of them being withheld from the public. Political considerations, I am certain, played a role in the censuring of the remaining titles.

However, it is easy given the first section of this novel as well as its *denouement,* to understand Watson's reluctance at having this particular case published. Although I am guessing here – a practice Holmes would certainly frown upon – I have to believe that the good doctor was every bit as concerned with keeping this tale from the public as was Holmes. His motivations may have been many – concern for his wife, regard for his own reputation as a practicing physician and perhaps, to a lesser degree, personal embarrassment. There was also another pressing concern arguing against its publication, which I hope shall become apparent as you read.

Obviously, the concern for Holmes' reputation also factored into the decision to hold back this tale. Certainly, publishing it in *The Strand Magazine* immediately following its conclusion was out of the question – for any number of other reasons.

Like so many aspects of the Canon, speculation as to a motive in a particular case such as this one may well lead us down a rabbit-hole from which we emerge some time later with much the same opinions as when we entered – although it must be admitted the time spent in such places is always fascinating.

That being said, I leave it you, dear readers, to form your own judgments. I just hope that you enjoy this tale as much as I do.

– Richard T. Ryan

Prologue

More than two decades have passed since I last read this story. Knowing that it could not see the light of day for many years, if at all, I set it aside, but I never forgot about it. In fact, there are events in this book that haunt me to this very day and will no doubt continue to do so.

When I first set to paper the events that transpired more than twenty years ago, I distinctly recall having serious reservations about possibly bringing it to light in my lifetime or that of my friend, Sherlock Holmes. Although those fears have been allayed to some degree, they have not been totally erased.

The case was certainly one of the strangest that challenged my friend, and only an intellect as keen as his could have discerned the truth hidden away amongst a labyrinth of distractions. Holmes oft-repeated dictum: "There is nothing more deceptive than an obvious fact," was certainly borne out in the events that began in the spring and continued to play out over the summer and the autumn of 1889.

Should anyone ever read this – a consideration of which I have serious doubts – you will notice various discrepancies between several of the events of this tale and some of my later narratives. There was never an intent to deceive, dear reader. In those later tales, I was merely exercising a bit of dramatic licence with regard to a few of the facts. When writing those tales, I had the present story in hand. As this tale remained moribund, facing

1

an uncertain future, I forged ahead and decided to take a few liberties.

In those few instances, my intent was always to entertain while at the same time demonstrating the almost preternatural abilities of my friend, Sherlock Holmes.

At any rate, I extend the olive branch and beg for your forgiveness. My ardent hope is that you enjoy this depiction of Holmes' ratiocinations and forgive the failings – both literary and moral – of the man entrusted with serving as his Boswell.

– John H. Watson, M.D.

"The greatest deception men suffer
is from their own opinions."

– Leonardo da Vinci

"All men profess honesty as long as they can.
To believe all men honest would be folly.
To believe none so is something worse."

– John Quincy Adams

"Chess is the gymnasium of the mind."

– Blaise Pascal

3

Chapter 1 – 1 July, 1889

For some odd reason, I remember every detail of that day quite vividly. Part of the recollection may stem from the fact that Holmes had just finished working on an adventure which I subsequently titled "The Adventure of the Naval Treaty," and I was assembling my notes on that rather memorable affair.

My wife had departed the previous day to tend to an ailing cousin in Scotland, and I had taken up residence in my old rooms at Baker Street, for what I expected to be her rather lengthy absence. It was a warm and humid Monday, and the time was exactly 11:44 a.m. when I heard the front door bell ring. Whoever was calling was impatient, as the ring was repeated twice more before Mrs. Hudson had the opportunity to move from the kitchen – where she was preparing lunch for Holmes and me. Since she normally answers before even a second ring is required, I felt that the matter on which the caller had come to see Holmes, for I was certain it was for him, must be one of some urgency.

"Someone would appear to be in quite a hurry to see you?" I said.

"Oh," remarked Holmes, who had been working at his chemistry table and was so immersed in his test tubes and retorts that he had been oblivious to the repeated sounds of the bell.

The footfalls ascending the stairs were quite rapid, and I can only assume that our caller was taking them two at a time. When a heavy hand struck the door thrice in succession, Holmes, who had now shifted his attention from his experiment to focus on the sounds emanating from the door, looked at me, and said, "I wonder what could possibly bring Inspector Lestrade here on a Monday and in a mood that seemingly will brook no nonsense."

"Come in, Inspector," he called across the room.

I was not surprised when Lestrade entered. I had seen Holmes perform similar feats of deduction on countless occasions. Normally not the neatest man to begin with, Lestrade, I must say, looked positively disheveled as he stood there, quite obviously out of breath and seemingly quite flustered. "Thank goodness, you are here, Mr. Holmes," he wheezed. "I don't know what I should have done if you weren't."

"Take a moment to catch your breath, Inspector," I advised. "A glass of water, perhaps?"

At the same time, Holmes said, "What on Earth is the matter, Lestrade? And why are you working instead of tending to your garden? I was under the impression you were supposed to be taking a short holiday."

"I'm covering today for Inspector Finley; his daughter is getting married in Ireland on Saturday. Each inspector volunteered for one day to give him some extra time off to help with the preparations and the travel."

"Well, you will congratulate Finley for me when you see him. He's a good man."

"I certainly will," replied Lestrade. "Now to the matter at hand. There has been a murder, or at least I am pretty certain there has."

"That's rather a lot to take in, and while I am in my element dealing with *apparent* contradictions, I must say this doesn't appear to be one. Either you have a murder or you do not.

"Do you have a dead body?" Holmes continued.

Lestrade nodded and said, "Of course, we do."

"But you are uncertain regarding the actual cause of death?"

"You hit the mark there, Mr. Holmes. As far as we can tell from a cursory examination, there were no wounds on the body. However, there are at least two possible causes of death which seem readily apparent."

"And have you identified these potential causes?"

"Yes, sir. Asphyxiation or possibly starvation."

"My word," I exclaimed.

"We expect to know for certain after a post mortem has been conducted, Doctor, but for the moment, it appears as though it could have been either one – possibly both in concert."

"Either way, that's an agonizing death," I offered.

"Where was the body found, Lestrade?"

"As you know, Mr. Holmes, they have been working on Tower Bridge for more than three years now."

"I am all too well aware of that, Inspector. Given the rate of progress, I expect they will be working on it for at least three more years, quite possibly longer."

"For much of the past month, all of the workers have been concentrating on the Southwark side as there were some unexpected difficulties with that tower, apparently.

"As a result the tower on the north side of the river has languished and been vacant for some three weeks.

"At any rate, when the crews reported back to the north tower this morning, one of them noticed a section of wall which seemed out of place. When they examined it, it didn't line up with the specifications, and after studying it carefully, the foreman considered the masonry work to be substandard.

"He had one of the men pry out a brick; as a result, they discovered that it was more a façade than an actual section of wall. Reaching inside, the foreman felt cloth, so they decided to take down part of the section and see what it concealed. That's when they discovered the body."

"You know, Lestrade, this sounds a great deal like that short story, 'The Cask of Amontillado,' by Mr. Edgar Allan Poe," I offered.

"Indeed, it does," replied Lestrade, "but that's not the strangest thing."

"There's more to this macabre tale?" asked Holmes.

"Yes, sir. The body is that of a man. If I had to guess – and given the state of the corpse, I'd just be guessing – I would say he was about six feet tall, perhaps 40 years old, clean-shaven, with a full head of very dark brown hair."

"I don't suppose anyone matching that description has been reported missing," I ventured.

"Not as far as I know, Doctor, but we have just begun our investigation. So something may turn up."

"The proximity of the bridge to the Tower of London is rather suggestive in that it sounds as though this man might well have been a prisoner of some sort," I added.

"Any idea how long he has been in there?"

"We are hoping the coroner will be able to narrow it down, Doctor, but as a guess, I would say at least two weeks, perhaps three, possibly a bit longer."

"Tell me, Inspector, what was he wearing?" asked Holmes, rejoining the conversation.

"He had on a grey suit with a proper waistcoat, a white shirt and a dark blue cravat. However, the cravat had been removed and tied around his mouth as a gag. I should also mention that both his hands and feet were bound."

"That is rather important," remarked Holmes, adding, "It suggests he was alive when the wall was built."

"We believe he was, but we cannot say for certain, which is why I said I was unsure if it is a case of murder or simply hiding a body."

"The bonds and gag argue for the former," said Holmes, who continued, "Can you tell me anything about his boots?"

"Truth be told, I believe they were black, but I really didn't take much notice of them."

I saw Holmes bristle a bit and he responded rather coolly, "The colour is immaterial. I meant the shape they are in, for they may well tell me where this man has been. Obviously, you have a murdered man on your hands. But why come to me, when you have just discovered the body?"

"That's what I've been trying to tell you, Mr. Holmes, but you and Doctor Watson kept putting me off with all your questions."

"My apologies, Inspector," murmured Holmes, without the least bit of contrition in his voice. "Please continue."

"As you might expect, the man's wallet was missing, and he carried no papers that might help identify him that we could discover. However, tucked away in the breast pocket of his jacket was a small piece of paper that whoever killed him must have overlooked."

"And, pray tell, what did it say Inspector?"

"Printed on it in neat block letters were the words: 221B BAKER STREET."

Chapter 2

"That is indeed most curious," replied Holmes. "I don't believe I have ever encountered a case of true immuration." Then speaking more to himself than us, he continued, "I suppose one could argue that Brunton was immured – although that was in large part his own doing."

At the time I had no idea, who this Brunton fellow might be, and before I could ask, Lestrade interrupted, "Immuration?"

"Come now, Inspector. Even you have had some Latin, certainly! From *im* or 'in' and *murrus* or 'wall.' Literally, the word means being 'walled in.'"

Having finished his brief linguistic dissertation, Holmes asked Lestrade, "You will notify us as to the time and place of the post mortem?"

Seeing that Holmes had made the decision to involve himself in the matter, Lestrade readily agreed to contact us with all the particulars about the coroner's examination. "Would you like to come to the bridge now, Mr. Holmes?"

"Between the workers and the policemen, I am certain that anything that might have been revealed has already been trampled underfoot.

"No, Inspector. I will wait to hear from you, and do take special care with his clothing. We may yet be able to learn a great deal about this man from his attire."

After promising to heed Holmes' advice regarding the man's garments, the inspector departed in a much better frame of mind.

After hearing the front door close, I waited for Holmes to say something, but he seemed more intent on returning to his unfinished experiment. Deciding to seize the initiative, I said, "Whether it be asphyxiation, starvation or, as is more likely, dehydration, it is still a most agonizing death."

My words appeared to give him pause and after considering, he explained, "Truly, Watson, but still immuration has a long and colourful history. Vestal virgins in ancient Rome were buried alive if it was believed they had violated their vow of chastity. Thieves in Persia have been immurated for centuries; in fact, it is still practiced today in some of the more remote areas of that region."

"But Holmes, this is the nineteenth century – almost the twentieth?"

"Yes, and ignorance still holds sway in many parts of the world. For example, there are any number of countries – Greece, Serbia, Albania – where there are tales and ballads containing as a theme the sacrifice of a human being to ensure the strength of a building. In Japan, in particular, people were often sacrificed and immured in bridges in an effort to make certain they did not collapse."

"You don't think that is what has happened here?"

"I don't think anything yet, my friend. It is too soon to even consider formulating a motive. We have no data. All we have for the moment is Lestrade's rather incomplete report of a bound body wearing a grey suit, white shirt, blue cravat and boots of some color – possibly black. Other than that, we are ignorant."

"But surely you must have some ideas."

"No, Watson, I am not even going to think about this case – if indeed it becomes a case – until we know a great deal more. Now, I think we have put off enjoying the lunch that Mrs. Hudson has prepared for us long enough."

Holmes was as good as his word and refused to say anything else about the potential case. I tried to draw him into conversation two or three times, but finally I realised I was wasting my breath and conceded this round to my friend.

The afternoon passed quickly and after supper, I decided that rather than pursuing the matter, I would spend the evening at my club. Unfortunately, the body in the Tower Bridge was the only thing anyone seemed to want to talk about, and no one would believe that Holmes had not yet developed any theories about the deceased.

Although I am a sociable individual by nature, this was one time where I wished I were a member of the Diogenes Club – a place where I knew no one would bother me with questions or inane theories. After an hour of incessant badgering, I could tolerate no more, and I returned home to discover Holmes had gone out.

I decided to read and wait up for my friend, but by eleven o'clock I was nodding off, and after perusing the same paragraph four times, I decided my vigil was to be a fruitless one, so I turned in.

As I was lying in bed, I found myself wondering if any structures in London had been constructed with bodies within their walls. I cannot say for certain exactly when I finally fell asleep, but I do know that it was long after my head first hit the pillow.

Despite my restlessness, I awoke the next morning feeling oddly refreshed. I joined Holmes at the breakfast table where he had ensconced himself behind his copy of *The London Times*. Gazing at the front page where the headline "Body in Tower Bridge" had been positioned so it could not fail to attract the reader's attention, I remarked, "I see the Tower Bridge story has captured the editor's fancy."

"Yes, indeed," replied Holmes from behind the paper. "Of course, there are a great many lurid details – most of which I am certain are specious – as well as an ample supply of idle speculation. I do hope this sensationalism is just a temporary fad with what passes for journalism today."

As I was about to reply, there was a knock on the door. Before I could say anything, Holmes called out, "Come in, Mrs. Hudson."

Our landlady stepped into the room and said, "This just arrived for you in the morning post, Mr. Holmes." With that she handed my friend an envelope, curtseyed and departed as quietly as she had entered.

"What have we here?" said Holmes as he examined the envelope. "The paper is quite dear and it has been typed – on one of the new Remington No. 2 machines I should think." Showing me the envelope, he continued, "Note that the machine is able to produce both upper and lower cases letters – a distinct improvement upon the original Sholes and Glidden Type-Writer."

Slitting open the envelope with a penknife, Holmes extracted a single sheet of cream-coloured paper which had been folded in two. After opening it, he read it over silently two or three times and then passed it to me, saying, "What do you make of this, Watson."

I looked at the note, which read:

Dear Mr. Holmes,

If it is agreeable, I should like to call upon you at 6 o'clock tomorrow evening. If the hour is inconvenient, please tell me when you are free, and I will attempt to adjust my schedule to accommodate yours. I will tell you that my evenings are free so that would be easier for me. Please believe me when I say this is a matter of some urgency – perhaps even life or death. You may contact me at the Savoy Hotel, Room 316. I look forward to meeting with you and pray that you will be able to assist me in my hour of need.

Sincerely yours,

Linda Reed

"Just on the basis of the letter, she would appear to be a refined young woman," I offered.

"Nothing else jumps out at you?"

"Well, she must be fairly well-off if she is staying at the Savoy, and given the tone she does appear rather desperate."

"Will you never tire of plucking the low-hanging fruit?" inquired Holmes. "Consider, why would a young woman type a letter rather than write it by hand? Bear in mind also, she is an excellent typist. There are no misspellings, and nothing has been erased or crossed out."

"Which tells you what?"

"That she is most probably a secretary here with her employer. She types for him or her and out of habit typed her missive to me. Add to that the fact that she wishes to see me at six o'clock or later in the evening and that tells me she is coming here after she has completed her duties during the day."

"My word! You don't miss much, do you?"

"It was all there for you to see as well."

15

The next day was overcast with intermittent showers which continued into the evening, and the gray skies matched my mood. I was quite busy at my practice – so much so that I had completely forgot about Holmes' appointment. I arrived at Baker Street around a quarter to six, tired and famished and thankful I had thought to take my umbrella.

"I was afraid you were going to be late," said Holmes as I entered our sitting room.

I almost said "Late for what?" but then I remembered the previous day's letter and caught myself. Instead I uttered, "I wouldn't have missed it."

Although Holmes gave me a curious look, he said nothing. After I had hung up my coat and settled into my chair, he offered, "I asked Mrs. Hudson to hold supper until seven. I think an hour should be more than sufficient to learn why Miss Reed has come to see us."

Inwardly I groaned at that pronouncement, but I knew how Holmes would eschew food whenever he was involved in a case. Secretly, I hoped I would dine at seven, but I feared such might not be the case.

Some ten minutes later, I heard the bell ring and shortly after that Mrs. Hudson knocked on our door.

"Yes, Mrs. Hudson?" said Holmes.

Our landlady entered the room and said, "A young lady is here to see you, sir. A Miss Linda Reed – she says she has an appointment."

"Indeed, she does," replied Holmes. "If you would be so kind as to show her up."

A minute later, a young woman entered. When she did, both Holmes and I stood up. She was tall and slender with long auburn hair. She was sensibly dressed and she carried an umbrella. She gazed at Homes then at me then back at Holmes and then again at me. Finally, she set her gaze on Holmes and said, "I presume you are Mr. Sherlock Holmes."

"I am," replied he, "and this is my colleague, Dr. John Watson. I see you had some difficulty in securing a carriage and were forced to make do with a dog cart."

"That's true. I suppose with ..." and then her voice trailed off as she realised the full import of Holmes' remark. "How could you have possibly known?"

"Although your skirt is wet in several places on the left side – presumably from the wind blowing the rain – your sleeves and shoes are quite dry. Obviously, the umbrella protected your arms, and I'm sure you kept your feet as far back as possible under the seat which explains why they are clean and dry. Next time, ask the driver for a blanket. They often carry them but some of them will provide them only when requested."

"I will and thank you."

"Now, how may I be of assistance?"

"My brother, John, has gone missing. He came to London a little more than a month ago. The first week he was here, he wrote me daily and then suddenly all communication ceased. It is not like John to stop writing for such a prolonged period."

"When you say he came to London little more than a month ago, do you have an exact date when he arrived here?"

"He asked our employer – we both work for Baron Friedrich Leighton at Brucastle Abbey in Lincolnshire – for a week off. It was the twenty-ninth of May, two days after my birthday, that he departed for London. I last heard from him exactly one week later – the fifth of June."

"And why was your brother coming to London?"

"I cannot say for certain, Mr. Holmes. I believe he had stumbled across something that had upset him greatly, and he had made certain inquiries around the village. The only thing I know for sure is that he was determined to get to the bottom of what was troubling him."

Chapter 3

As the conversation progressed, we learned Miss Reed was employed as the personal secretary of Lady Elizabeth Leighton, the younger sister of Baron Friedrich Leighton, while her brother had been employed as the stable master. They had followed their parents, who had worked for the previous owners and stayed on with Baron Leighton, into service at Brucastle Abbey and were quite content there – until recently.

"As I said, Mr. Holmes, John became aware of something, and it troubled him greatly. He refused to discuss it with anyone, not even me. After a week or two of fussing and fuming, he decided to come to London to seek assistance and to use his words, 'Do a little investigating.' I wish I could be of more help. You will try to find him, sir? I will pay you anything."

I glanced at Holmes, who imperceptibly shook his head indicating no. But then turning to the young woman, he said, "I promise you, Miss Reed, that I will do everything in my power to locate your brother." Holmes then asked her to describe her brother. As you might expect, her description was quite close to the body discovered in the Tower Bridge.

After she had finished, Holmes asked a few more questions and then repeated his assertion. Her relief was almost palpable. "Thank you, Mr. Holmes, and you as well, Dr. Watson. I will be in London for two more days and then we are returning to Brucastle Abbey. Opening her bag, she pulled out a sheet of paper. "Here is my address in Lincolnshire. I believe you have my room number at the Savoy. Thank you again, Mr. Holmes, and I look forward to hearing from you."

After she departed I looked at Holmes and said, "Is there a reason you didn't tell her?"

"I didn't tell her because I do not know for certain. Do I think the body from the bridge is that of her brother? It would be foolish to think otherwise, but until we know for certain, let us keep our own counsel."

Although I was disappointed, I could certainly see the logic in Holmes' argument. "So then, what's to be done?"

"We wait to hear from Lestrade about the post mortem on the body. In the interim, I shall do a little research into Baron Friedrich Leighton." So saying, he pulled down one of his many indices from the bookshelf, and after filling his pipe, he began to thumb through it.

After a few minutes, he looked up and said, "Although I have a fair number of entries filed under L, I cannot find any reference to Baron Leighton. Perhaps the estate has made its way into my collection."

He pulled down another volume and began to read. After several minutes, he remarked, "This Brucastle Abbey has quite the history. It dates back to the twelfth century when it was first constructed. It was later enlarged and modernised at the beginning of the sixteenth century." He chuckled, "I suppose we should take the word 'modernised' quite loosely."

He then continued, "The estate was seized from the Cook family, who were practicing Catholics, in 1590 by agents acting on behalf of Queen Elizabeth I. After executing Lord Cook and imprisoning the rest of his family, the Queen then presented the abbey to one of her more ardent supporters, the third Earl of Sommersby, in whose family it remained until credit problems forced them to sell it to Baron Leighton in 1876."

Having warmed to his task, he began exchanging one book for another. An act he repeated several times before he settled on one volume. After perusing it for several minutes, he exclaimed, "Ah, here it is, an article from the *Lincolnshire Standard*, dated 15 March, 1886: 'Woman Missing at Brucastle Abbey.'" He then read in silence for a few minutes before looking up at me. "What a strange tale!"

"What does it say, Holmes."

"Apparently, a young woman by the name of Constance Palmer, a guest at Brucastle Abbey, went missing in the middle of the night. The entire household had turned in, and no one heard anything. The next morning, she did not come down for breakfast. Her bedroom door was locked, and after it was broken down, there was no sign of her. All her possessions were there, but the woman had, and here I quote, 'apparently vanished into thin air.'"

"What do you suppose happened?"

"I have no idea, but as I am looking into Baron Leighton anyway, I shall devote some time to that matter as well. After all people don't just vanish 'into thin air.' At the same time, if you are so disposed, you might make a few discreet inquiries at your club and see if anyone in your circle is acquainted with the Baron."

"I have no plans for this evening, so unless you have need of my services, I will attend to it straight away."

"Splendid! And while you are doing that, I shall conduct a few interrogations of my own."

I was pleased that only one or two people asked about the body at Tower Bridge; however, despite my best efforts, I learned little at my club. Although almost everyone I spoke to had heard of Baron Leighton, very few knew anything substantial about him – and no one at the club knew him personally. The only solid fact I could gather, and I heard this from three different members, was that the Baron was renowned for his weekend soirees. Although none of the men had ever been invited, they had all heard from friends about the weekend gatherings at Brucastle Abbey, which appeared to be the stuff of legend.

I returned home feeling as though I had wasted the better part of an evening and hoping Holmes had fared better. I entered our rooms and found my friend sitting in his chair, puffing on his old and oily black clay pipe.

The significance of that particular pipe was not lost on me, and I wondered what he had discovered that had made him seek the solace of his old "counselor."

"Ah, Watson. Nothing to report, I see."

I had no idea how he had ascertained that fact, but I was in no mood to encourage his showmanship. So I merely nodded and said, "Right you are." I could see he was disappointed that I had not taken the bait, but I carried on despite my misgivings.

"I gather your evening has been somewhat more productive than mine."

"Only slightly," he replied, "however, I am waiting for several wires which may push things along a bit. Hopefully, we will know more tomorrow."

"Yes, but you said your evening was 'slightly' better than mine. Therefore I can conclude some tidbit of knowledge has come your way, presumably about Baron Leighton."

Holmes gazed at me with what I thought was a hint of admiration. "You are getting quite good at this, Watson. At any rate, I visited my brother at the Diogenes Club."

I recalled that it was only the previous year that I had become aware of the fact that Holmes even had a brother. "And what did Mycroft have to say?"

"He seemed to recall a case from several years ago in which Baron Leighton was tangentially involved with the accidental hunting death of a young nobleman who had a promising career in the government."

"Accidents do happen," I offered.

"Yes, they do. However, those involving Baron Leighton in any way always appear to be fatal."

"Holmes, you don't mean …"

"I don't mean anything yet, my friend. I have no real data at present, merely second-hand stories, rumours and innuendo."

"Speaking of rumours," I countered, "while no one at my club would admit to knowing Baron Leighton, three fellows with whom I played a few games of whist all claimed to be aware of some rather lavish soirees that the Baron is known to host on weekends."

"Your sources are solid, old friend. Mycroft passed along a similar comment, so the questions would seem to be: How often does the Baron host these merry-making festivities and how does one go about getting invited?"

"You don't mean that you would go? Wouldn't that be tipping off the Baron that you were interested in his affairs?"

"I might not go – at least not as myself, certainly – but you could surely attend."

"Holmes, you can't be serious," I spluttered.

"Watson, I am beginning to sense a malevolence here. Whether it resides in Baron Leighton himself or someone close to him has yet to be determined. But we have a death and a disappearance in close proximity to the Baron, as well as a second death that appears to be connected to him at least peripherally. I am hopeful even you can begin to see the outline of a pattern."

"I see three events separated by a number of years. Are they connected? Perhaps. Unfortunately, I lack your perception and cannot ascertain any outline as of now."

"Consider, Watson, a woman disappears in the middle of the night from a locked room? Is that not an unusual occurrence?"

"It is," I admitted.

"A man is discovered walled up in one of the towers for a bridge. Does that not strike you as peculiar?"

"It does."

"And a young man, otherwise healthy, perishes in a hunting accident – having been shot by accident, apparently. Certainly that's a common enough occurrence," he concluded with a hint of sarcasm.

"Dash it all, Holmes. You make it all sound so sinister."

"Perhaps it is, and perhaps it is merely coincidence – although I am inclined not to believe in the latter."

"So then what will you do?"

"Not me, old man. This is most definitely a case where I will require your assistance. So to rephrase your question: What will *we* do? Truthfully, I am not yet certain, but I will look into the owner, the residents and the employees of Brucastle Abbey. What I will discover has yet to be determined. Now, would you care for a nightcap before bed?"

As we sipped our brandy, I looked at my friend and said, "Just once, I'd like you to come a cropper with your suspicions."

"There have been many times when I wished I were wrong as well. Unfortunately, when I see an injustice, I must act. And when I sense a wrong, I cannot help but attempt to right it."

As we sat there smoking and enjoying our drinks, I had no idea, at the time, how prophetic Holmes' words would prove to be.

Chapter 4

As the days passed and we moved towards the close of summer, I found myself quite busy at my surgery. After returning from Scotland, my wife, Mary, had fallen ill herself and caring for her filled the remainder of my days and nights.

Weeks went by and I had heard nary a word from Holmes. Such instances were not uncommon, and I had learned to take his prolonged absences in stride. I had followed with particular interest a murder case in the Lambeth section. When the perpetrator was arrested, Fleet Street was lavish in its praise of "Scotland Yard's Finest," Inspectors Lestrade and Gregson. However, to anyone who knew what to look for, a careful analysis of the facts would have revealed that, as might be expected, Holmes had been instrumental in bringing the ne'er-do-well to justice, and in his customary manner, eschewing the credit, instead, passing it along to his friends.

Distracted as I was by so many pressing concerns – my wife's condition, my burgeoning practice as well as the continuing exploits of my old friend – thoughts of Baron Leighton and the body in the Tower Bridge had slowly faded. So I was rather surprised when one evening in late August, there was a gentle knock on my front door. I opened it to find Holmes standing there, holding of all things a small basket and a bouquet of flowers.

He must have seen the puzzled expression on my face, for he quickly remarked, "Mrs. Hudson asked me to convey her best wishes to you and your wife for a speedy recovery. She insisted that I bring these along."

I took the basket from Holmes and placed the flowers in a vase. As I arranged the blooms, I glanced at my old friend. I couldn't tell whether he was embarrassed at not having brought something himself or simply at sea over how to conduct himself under these unusual, for him at least, circumstances. Knowing the man as I did, I decided it was the latter.

"It's so good to see you, Holmes. That appears to have been quite a nasty bit of work in Lambeth, but I see you managed to cover Lestrade and Gregson in glory."

"It was quite a simple case, actually. Once I learned that the footman was deeply in debt due to his misadventures on the turf, it all fell together rather nicely."

In spite of myself, I laughed. "Holmes, I have had more than my share of miserable days with the horses, but I've never killed anyone."

"True, true, but then to the best of my knowledge you have never been in debt to the tune of £500 to a rather notorious bookmaker, nor were you ever named as a beneficiary in anyone's will. I believe the sum was £3,000 – more than enough to drive a desperate man to commit murder."

"But how was it accomplished? And why was it not detected initially?"

"Well into her dotage, Mrs. Simpson was also a known hypochondriac. She was already taking digitalis in small doses on the advice of one of her many physicians. Unfortunately, the rapacious footman had surreptitiously placed a number of very strong digitalis tablets among the plethora of medicines she consumed every day, so it was just a matter of time."

"That's dastardly but brilliant! How did you arrive at that conclusion?"

"Her sister, Agnes Bencher, suspected something was amiss. She had been to see Mrs. Simpson two days before her death. At that time the victim seemed generally well although rather nauseous and lethargic. She also complimented Mrs. Bencher on the distinctive shade of her dress."

"So far, I can see nothing unusual."

"That's because I haven't finished. Mrs. Bencher was wearing a light blue dress, but her sister said she thought it quite a striking shade of yellow."

"Indeed. People suffering from digitalis poisoning will often see objects as either green or yellow. Bravo, Holmes." He smiled and so I continued, "But you couldn't prove digitalis poisoning on the basis of a misperceived color."

"Certainly not, and therein rests the value of a thorough examination of the crime scene. After being contacted by the victim's sister the day of Mrs. Simpson's death, I examined her room the following morning and was fortunate enough to spy two tablets in a chink in the floor under her bed. One was a patent headache remedy, but the other, much to my good fortune, was one of the more potent digitalis tablets.

"Some inquiries into the backgrounds of the servants, coupled with visits to all of the nearby chemists soon pointed me to the footman. In turn, I sicced Lestrade and Gregson on him, and justice was served."

"Are there any other cases of note of which I am unaware?"

"None at the moment. Although you haven't yet asked, you should know I am still looking into Baron Leighton, and I have made a few more discoveries about the nobleman in question."

"Have you? Pray tell what have you learned."

"I know that until fairly recently, perhaps a decade ago, Baron Leighton was a social non-entity. Although he comes from an old Norman family, he had been a social outlier. Somehow he and the Prince of Wales struck up a friendship and that bond is what has provided the Baron with no small degree of social cachet which he has since augmented considerably. Given what I have learned about Leighton, it is not difficult to imagine the types of favours he must have done for the Prince."

"Holmes, do take care. Edward will no doubt be our next monarch."

"One can only hope that when that comes to pass, he is no longer the man he is today."

"Surely, he cannot be as bad as his reputation. You know yourself how the ink-stained wretches in the press enjoy sensationalizing everything."

"No, Watson, he is not nearly as bad as his reputation – he is, on occasion, worse. However, the Prince is not our concern. It's this cutpurse whom he has elevated to his social circle who perturbs me.

"In researching Leighton, I have learned he has a rather checkered history. Early in his life he escaped a few close brushes with the law, but since having acquired his title, he appears to have walked the straight and narrow.

"What's I find most interesting is that while he maintains his country estate, a pied-à-terre in London and frequently throws lavish parties, he has no discernable source of income."

"You don't suppose he is blackmailing the Prince?"

"I don't think the Prince would tolerate being extorted. No, I think Baron Leighton comes by his money in an altogether different way."

"Are you going to share this information or make me guess?'

"When last we spoke of the Baron, we had two unusual deaths linked to him as well as the disappearance of a young woman."

"Yes, I recall all too well."

"You were unable to attend the post mortem for the man in Tower Bridge. He had been walled in alive, and died, as you suggested, of dehydration. As we suspected, he was the brother of the charming Miss Reed. Although the killer attempted to remove all forms of identification, Mr. Reed had a most distinctive feature that was not readily apparent but came to light during the examination."

"Do tell."

"He had an unusual birthmark on the inside of his right calf."

"And from that you were able to obtain a positive identification?"

"Yes and it's fortunate that birthmark was hidden, or I am afraid we might still be fumbling about looking for data to help us with this case, for I am certain the body would have been concealed in a manner that guaranteed it would never be found."

"You confirmed this with the sister?"

"Yes, I think she realised her brother's fate when I asked her if he had any unusual scars or other distinguishing features."

"How did she take the news?"

"I think it was a mixed blessing. At least she knows what became of her brother. With Lestrade's assistance, I managed to spare her most of the gory details – and then I swore her to secrecy."

"But how does this lead us to Baron Leighton?"

"I have learned that in the past decade the Baron has been associated with no fewer than nine people who have died under mysterious circumstances or else disappeared entirely."

"Holmes, you are not suggesting ..."

"No, Watson," he said cutting me off, "I am stating that in my opinion Baron Friedrich Leighton is nothing more than a paid assassin."

"My word, Holmes! That is quite an allegation. I do hope that you can prove it."

"Not just yet, old friend, which is why you are the only one with whom I am sharing my suspicions."

"I appreciate the vote of confidence, but I don't see how I can help."

"I have the beginnings of a plan. Admittedly, it is still in the rudimentary stages, but with your cooperation, I hope to bring it to fruition."

There was something in Holmes' voice which I found unusual – a certain reticence if you will. As you might expect, I found it slightly off-putting. I had lived with the man for years, and we had risked our lives together on occasions too numerous to recall. To suddenly find my friend hesitant and uncertain was something I thought I would never see.

After a rather prolonged, and I might add awkward, silence, I finally said, "Out with it, man. Tell me what it is you are thinking."

What followed next almost defies description. When he had finished, he was once again the Holmes I knew. The bandage had been ripped away. Although I found his ideas distasteful in the extreme, his last words – "Watson, he has eluded detection for more than a decade. With your help, we may finally bring his career to an abrupt halt. Should you decline, and I will certainly understand if you do, there is no telling how many more people will fall victim to this evil man…" – convinced me that I would have to shunt my feelings aside and join my friend in bringing down the curtain on this unseen reign of terror.

"What you ask will give me no end of pain, and I'm not certain that I am the best man for the task, but if you think I can pull it off, I shall give it my best effort."

"Good old Watson, I knew I could depend on you."

Chapter 5

I did not hear from Holmes for several weeks following our conversation. I assumed he was up to his usual Machiavellian tricks – maneuvering people and creating situations to suit his own ends. Suddenly, one night about eight o'clock, there was a knock on the front door. I answered it, and found a messenger there.

"Are you Dr. John Watson?" he asked reading the name from the envelope.

"I am," I replied.

"Then this is for you." He handed me a plain white envelope, and in turn, I handed the lad a few coppers. He thanked me and then scampered off down the street.

From upstairs, I heard my wife call down in a worried voice, "Who is it, John?"

Looking at the familiar scrawl on the envelope, I replied, "Just a note from Holmes. I have yet to read it, but I will tell you what it says after I do."

Watson,

> *The game progresses. If you are free,*
>
> *please join me for supper tomorrow night*
>
> *at 7 as we have much to discuss.*

> *S.H.*

When I told Mary that Holmes had requested I join him for dinner the following evening, she encouraged me to go: "You haven't seen him in quite some time, and you deserve a break from caring for me. I'll ask Alice to stay late; I'm certain she won't mind. She can prepare dinner for me as well."

Struck by her selflessness, I felt no small amount of guilt at leaving her alone, but I knew that she would have spoken to me in even stronger terms had I made her aware of the doings of Baron Leighton.

The next evening I made my way to my old rooms. When I rang the bell, I was greeted warmly by Mrs. Hudson. After we had exchanged pleasantries, she concluded by saying, "It's just not the same here without you, Doctor."

I thanked her for her kind words and made my way up the stairs. Out of politeness, I knocked, and when I heard Holmes bellow, "Come in, Watson," I knew I was home.

We enjoyed a meal of mutton chops with mint sauce, roasted potatoes and runner beans. While my housekeeper, Alice, was accomplished in the kitchen, her skill paled beside that of my former landlady.

When we had finished supper and were enjoying brandy and cigars, Holmes turned to me, his eyes sparkling with excitement, and said, "I do hope that you are free a month from this Friday."

"I have no idea, but if it is important, I will adjust my schedule. What do you have planned?"

"I have secured you an invitation to Baron Leighton's soiree that weekend."

"You can't be serious," I exclaimed.

"It took a great deal of work and more than a few palms had to be greased, but it has all been arranged."

"But Holmes, I do not move in the same circles as the Baron. What am I to say or do?"

"Watson, you sell yourself short. You are an accomplished medical man with a thriving practice; moreover, you are a literary lion."

I laughed in spite of myself. "My practice puts bread on the table and the stories of our adventures allow me a few extra creature comforts, but a literary lion? No one will believe that."

"Watson, whether they will admit it or not, everyone reads your stories. You have far more of a following than you perhaps realise. In fact, were I you, I should consider asking quite a bit more for the stories you produce in the future. Trust me when I say, you are without peer in your chosen métier," he paused before concluding, "just as I am in mine."

Inwardly, I chuckled because even when the situation had little or naught to do with him, Holmes always managed to find a way to insinuate himself into the conversation. Buoyed by my friend's remarks and impressed by the gravity of the situation, I responded, "Tell me what it is you would like me to do."

"To begin with, tomorrow I want you to visit Henry Poole and Co. in Savile Row."

All too aware of the haberdasher's reputation, I exclaimed, "Holmes, I can't afford that type of luxury."

"Not to worry, old friend. It has all been arranged and paid for. Mr. Cundey, the proprietor, simply needs to take your measurements."

"For what? And who is paying for these goods?"

"I believe the order is for three suits – grey, navy and brown as well as six shirts of varying colors, socks, ties and boots. Oh yes, you will also be fitted for a dinner jacket. Might I suggest the short jacket which Mr. Poole designed for the Prince of Wales a while back?"

"And the bill? I am certain it will be considerable."

"As I said, it has been taken care of. Think of these goods as payment in kind for services rendered."

Suddenly, I realised there was a higher power at work here. At that time, I had a very limited knowledge of Holmes' brother, Mycroft. However, I suspected that given his position with the government, he had involved himself in this affair, perhaps in an effort to spare Prince Albert any embarrassment that might ensue were the Baron to be revealed as a murderer.

"And while I am away for the weekend?"

"Perhaps you can arrange with your neighbor to cover your practice?"

"That's easily done. And Mary?"

"Hopefully, she will be feeling well enough to visit her cousins in Scotland once again. If not, other arrangements can certainly be made."

"I should like her away from this business. From everything you have told me, Baron Leighton is a dangerous man, and he appears to have quite a long reach."

"Old friend, you have my word that Mrs. Watson will be protected at all times."

I knew in situations such as this that Holmes' word was his bond. "What time am I to see Mr. Cundey?"

Holmes laughed, "Any time in the afternoon. He will be expecting you."

The next afternoon I made my way to 15 Savile Road. Henry C. Poole was one of the city's oldest tailors with an impeccable reputation. The business had been founded in 1806 by John Poole who had left it to his son, Henry. When Henry passed away, his cousin, Samuel Cundey, had taken ownership.

Stepping into the shop, I was amazed at what a hum of activity it was. There were bolts of fabric everywhere, and several tailors were busy cutting and stitching. I gave my name and asked for Mr. Cundey. A few minutes later a rather unprepossessing gentleman, who was nevertheless the picture of sartorial splendor, introduced himself. "I am Samuel Cundey. I will be your personal tailor as long as you are a customer at Henry C. Poole, which I hope will be a very long time."

Mr. Cundey then went on to explain that under normal circumstances suits such as mine might take anywhere from ten to twelve weeks. "However, I understand we have but four weeks, so I will need you to be available for additional fittings and alterations as the garments progress."

I assured him that I would make myself available, and he then began measuring me. "As you are aware, the colors have been pre-selected," he said, "but they left it to you to determine the exact fabrics you would prefer."

I was overwhelmed by the number of choices, but eventually selected three different weights of wool, including a twill, a gabardine and an incredibly expensive merino which Cundey suggested. My adventures in haberdashery that afternoon could fill a small volume by themselves, so let me just say here that the end results were well worth the time spent on measurements and fittings.

During the entire month leading up to the gala at Baron Leighton's, I heard from Holmes but twice. To be honest, they were brief non-committal notes which said little. By contrast, I saw Mr. Cundey on at least eight different occasions.

Finally, the Monday before the soiree, I was awakened about midnight by a youngster who said his mother was in labour. I followed the boy who told me his family lived in Spitalfields. I wondered why he had come such a long way to summon me.

Surely, there were other physicians who lived closer. Perhaps my reputation is spreading, I thought.

Given the hour, I was fortunate enough to find a cab on Harley Street, and we headed for the East End with all the speed the driver could muster. Nearly an hour later, we turned onto Fournier Street, The boy led me into a ground-floor flat and said his mother's room was in the back.

I heard no cries from a woman in labour, and I began to suspect I was alone in the flat. I called out, but there was no answer, and I was beginning to wonder what I had got myself into when Holmes emerged from the rear room. "Ah, Watson, it is so good to see you. I only wish it were under more felicitous circumstances."

"Why the pretense, Holmes? What the devil is going on?"

"Pray take a seat, old friend." Reaching into a cupboard, Holmes brought out a decanter of brandy and two glasses. After pouring us both a drink, he said, "I do not relish what I am about to tell you, nor do I think you are going to enjoy hearing it. Sadly, there are some things in this world that are unavoidable, and this is one of them."

When he spoke next, I was astounded at the words he uttered.

Chapter 6

"I am absolutely certain, Watson, that you and your home are being watched."

"By whom? And to what end?"

"As I explained some time ago, Baron Leighton is not a man to be trifled with. If he suspects for even one second that you are at his home as an agent of mine, you will be in enormous danger."

"Yes, but our friendship is well-known."

"And for the foreseeable future, it must end. I did indicate that this might have to occur."

I nodded, recalling his plan and then asked, "Do you have something in mind? A public falling out at a restaurant, perhaps?"

"No, Watson. The Baron would never fall for such an obvious ploy. Better an extended cooling off period such as we have had. This way when people ask – and they will ask, you may be certain of that – you can just say that between your burgeoning practice and your wife's illness, you no longer have time to be at the beck and call of a self-styled 'consulting detective.' Let those around you draw their own conclusions."

"Is that why you summoned me in the middle of the night?"

"It was a matter of necessity, and everything about this visit has been carefully arranged. This is one of my little hidey-holes. The woman in the flat above, Mrs. O'Malley gave birth to a son yesterday afternoon. It was handled with a great deal of discretion, and she is willing to swear that you assisted with the birth, and the boy was born early this morning."

"Well that takes care of this evening, but what about the future? Suppose I need to contact you immediately. What if I learn something important this weekend?"

"Nothing will happen this weekend, I guarantee it. You simply need to enjoy yourself, regale those on hand with tales of our exploits, and when you find the timing propitious and the circumstances favourable, perhaps drop a disparaging remark or two about me."

"Holmes, I could never ..."

He cut me off. "We've discussed this, old man. You don't have to mean it; nevertheless, it must sound sincere. Choose your words carefully – after all, you are a writer. Remember, although it may sting to utter the words, you will be advancing the cause of justice. If I am correct, Leighton is a remorseless murderer, and it has fallen to us to stop this monster."

"I will do my best, Holmes."

"That is all anyone could ask. Now, be safe and do try to enjoy yourself. I have it on the best of sources that these soirees are not to be missed."

"And while I am off enjoying myself, what exactly will you be doing?"

"I have several pressing cases at the moment," he replied. "One of which involves one of the reigning houses of Europe which is facing a scandal that could well have international repercussions. You need not worry about me, old friend, I have a great deal to keep me busy."

The next few days were something of a haze. I went through the motions at my practice, but anyone who knew me could see that my heart wasn't in it because my mind was elsewhere. Truth be told, I was trying to imagine – much as I thought Holmes might – the various scenarios I might encounter during my stay at Brucastle Abbey.

The day before I left, I was having dinner with Mary, who, feeling better, was scheduled to depart the next evening from Euston for the Highlands – a few hours after my train to Lincolnshire. We were sitting, enjoying a comfortable silence as married couples are wont to do, when she suddenly turned to me and said, "John, promise me you will be careful."

"What on Earth do you mean?"

She looked at me and smiled. "I know that you and Mr. Holmes are working on something. I don't know what and honestly, I don't want to know. In fact, I don't want to talk about it or even think about it. All I want you to do is promise me that you will not take any unnecessary chances."

I started to reply, but she took her index finger and put it on my lips as a sign that I should remain silent. Looking at me with those beautiful eyes, she said, "Just promise."

All I could do was nod and curse myself for having caused this incredible woman any undue anxiety. She then bent over and kissed me gently and said, "Let's go to bed, shall we?"

I awoke the next morning at odds with myself. I was torn between my unabashed love for my wife and my sense of duty. In the end, I knew duty would carry the day, but that did little to prevent me from feeling like a wretch.

I had arranged with Dr. Mallory to cover my practice on Friday and through the weekend. As I was packing, Mary entered. Unable to help myself, I asked, "How did you know that Holmes and I were working on a case?"

"Oh John. You suddenly order yourself three new suits and a dinner jacket – all quite dear – not to mention the shirts, ties, stockings and boots, and you don't say a word. I should think anyone could have figured out something was going on."

"It's bad enough when Holmes does it. I hope you don't mean to make a habit of it." At that we both laughed. I asked her which suit she thought I should wear on the train, and she selected the brown – which is the one I would have chosen. After we dressed, I treated her to a farewell lunch at Simpson's and then we took a cab home where I collected my bags. I will not bore you with the details of our parting, but my heart was aching as she waved to me from the front porch of our home.

I resolved to bury my feelings and caught a cab to King's Cross Station. I had a first-class compartment all to myself, or so I thought. At the last minute, a man, perhaps a decade or so younger than myself, entered the compartment.

I nodded and resumed reading Henry James' "The Aspen Papers," a novella of which I am certain Holmes would never approve. The time passed quickly as did the tale and shortly before the conductor announced "Lincolnshire," I had finished the book.

As I placed the book in my bag, my compartment companion said, "Was it as good as people say? It certainly seemed to occupy your attention." I thought I detected a slight brogue in that very proper English accent.

"Quite," I replied. "But then Shelley has always been one of my favourite poets, and James certainly knows how to tell a tale..."

Without further urging he leaned forward, gazed at me intently, and intoned in a surprisingly rich baritone:

> *"My name is Ozymandias, King of Kings;*
> *Look on my Works, ye Mighty, and despair!"*

I was so taken aback by his unexpected declaration I was at a loss for words for a few seconds, during which time he stuck out his hand and said, "I'm Dennis Mannery and it is a pleasure to meet you..."

"Watson," I replied. "Dr. John Watson."

"Are you *the* Dr. Watson, the writer?"

"Guilty as charged."

"It is a pleasure to meet you. I do so look forward to your stories in *The Strand* each month."

As we descended from the train, I noticed a number of other rather fashionably dressed people disembarking. I wondered whether I should follow them, but almost as though he had read my thoughts, Mannery inquired. "Are you going to Baron Leighton's?"

"How did you know?"

"Your hesitation spoke volumes as does your attire. Are your bags marked Brucastle Abbey?"

After I had answered in the affirmative, my new friend said, "Then follow me." Walking through the station, I saw people from the train climbing into an array of carriages. "The Baron always provides transportation. Sometimes I think he hires every trap in this village and the next. The porters are given a little extra to make certain that no one's bag is misplaced or goes missing."

"Obviously then, it would appear this is not your first visit here?"

"Oh, heavens no," he explained as we climbed into a trap. I have known Freddy for some time. We are old friends. Truth be told, I have an open invitation, and I try never to miss his little get-togethers."

"Well as you guessed, this is my first visit and, quite frankly, I'm not certain how or why I was invited."

"Freddy has his ways," said Mannery. "He enjoys surrounding himself with beautiful and interesting people."

I replied, "Well then I must certainly fall into the latter category." As you might expect, Mannery laughed at my reply and said, "Given that self-deprecating sense of humor, I believe you are going to fit right in."

During our ride in the trap from the station, my new friend gave me a short history of Brucastle Abbey. He explained how the hall traced its origins back to the English Civil War and how legend had it Charles I had been held there for several days after surrendering at nearby Southwell.

"The building you will soon see is actually the third incarnation of the abbey, the first two having burned down. The present Brucastle Abbey is widely regarded as a masterpiece of high Gothic architecture. It was designed by Sir George Gilbert Scott, who also designed the Albert Memorial in Kensington. He added a façade and several rooms to the existing structures and the result is an inharmonious harmony or what Dr. Samuel Johnson might have termed a *concordia discours*." Truth be told, I was having difficulty feigning interest in my new friend's narrative. However, all that changed when we crested a hill, and I saw the abbey off in the distance.

"My word! What an incredible building!" I was stunned at the sudden appearance of this magnificent structure in the middle of the unsullied countryside.

As I was ruminating about the building, my thoughts were interrupted by Mannery who offered, "It really is a sight to behold. Does anything about it strike you as familiar, Doctor?"

Despite never having seen it before, there was something about it that had inspired a sense of *deja vu*. "Indeed," I replied, "but I can't quite put my finger on it."

"Sir George employed many of the design elements, albeit on a much larger scale – "

"From the façade of the Midland Grand Hotel at St. Pancras," I said, finishing his thought for him,

"You have a sharp eye, Doctor. Something tells me the Baron is going to enjoy your company."

"And I his, I hope."

When we arrived at the entrance to the abbey, there were several carriages in front of us, and we had to wait to be announced. I tried to give the driver a few coins before I alighted, but he told me, "Thank you, sir, but no. The Baron has taken care of everything."

I followed Mannery into the entrance hall where people were milling about, exchanging greetings in a cordial manner. It was obvious that most of these people were well-acquainted with one another, and I felt like even more of an outlier.

Finally, one gentleman said to Mannery, "Dennis, who is your new friend? I don't believe I've seen him here before."

"I'm sure you haven't, Tom. Dr. Watson, I'd like to introduce Thomas Edwardson, he is an architect of no small repute."

Edwardson looked at me and asked, "Are you *the* Dr. Watson? The one who writes about Sherlock Holmes?"

At the mention of Holmes' name, several people in the vicinity turned in our direction. "You must tell me about him," Edwardson enthused. "Is he as brilliant as you make him out to be?"

"He is certainly clever; there's no denying that." Before I was forced to continue, Mannery said, "You must excuse us, Tom. There are a number of people who are clamoring to meet Dr. Watson."

"Hopefully, we can continue this conversation at some other time," Edwardson threw after me.

As we walked away, Mannery said, "The man would have had you there for hours, and there are other people I'd like you to meet."

Mannery then proceeded to introduce me to an array of people, several of whom expressed sentiments similar to those the architect had tendered, and I replied to them all in a rather terse manner.

This might have gone on for quite a bit longer, but the sound of a tinkling bell silenced everyone in the hall. When things had quieted, a butler announced, "Afternoon tea is now being served in the library."

I followed Mannery as he made his way across the hall and into a library that had obviously been designed with an eye for comfort as well as taste. There were leather-covered chairs scattered about and nooks where one might ensconce oneself with a book. In the middle of the room two large trestle tables had been erected and they were overflowing with platters of small sandwiches, scones, and biscuits. The servants were pouring tea into bone china cups while others were pouring sherry into stemmed crystal goblets.

After perhaps thirty minutes had passed, the bell tinkled again, and the butler announced, "Dinner will be served at seven o'clock. Proper attire is requested."

"You did bring evening clothes," Mannery said, "otherwise, you might find yourself dining alone."

I laughed and said I had then added, "I am exhausted. I should like very much to rest a bit before dinner."

"Of course, of course," he replied. "Let's see where the Baron has ensconced you."

After speaking with the butler, whose name I learned was Goodacre, Mannery said, "The Baron must be quite taken with your work. You have a suite on the first floor." Goodacre then returned and handed me a key.

Mannery led me up the elaborate staircase and down a long hallway to a room on the right. As I opened the door and stepped inside, my new friend said, "I'll call for you about a quarter to seven." I thanked him and he then headed back down the hallway.

The room was as elegant as any in which I had ever stayed. If I didn't know it was a private estate, I would have sworn it was one of the better hotels in London or Paris. There was a large sitting area, with a cherrywood writing desk and chair by the window. There were also three other chairs, a settee and a coffee table. A basket filled with fruit graced the table as well as two bottles of wine – red and white – glasses, a jug of water and a small tray of cakes and other savories. The bedroom itself was quite roomy with a large four-poster bed, a dressing table and an *en suite* bath.

I had no idea how the Baron was making his money, but given everything that had transpired thus far, it was easy to see how he was spending it.

Chapter 7

I will not bore you with an abundance of details about my weekend at Brucastle Abbey. However, there are a few pertinent facts which I feel obliged to share. The group at the Abbey numbered about 40 people, and they appeared to come from all walks of life. Among others, I recognised one or two actors as well as two members of Parliament, and a promising young artist.

The food and drink were never-ending, and there were plenty of surprises. One of the most delightful revelations was a performance by a soprano named Lisa Delfini. Gifted with a thrilling voice, she entertained the guests after dinner on Saturday with an impromptu concert, the highlight of which was a stunning rendition of the *Ave Maria* from Verdi's *Otello*.

Oddly enough, despite several opportunities, I was able to speak to the Baron only once – when we were introduced by Mannery after dinner that first night. I expressed my gratitude for being invited. The Baron was the epitome of charm. He expressed admiration for my literary endeavours and then was called away.

The only other thing I noticed which seemed worthy of mention was that there seemed to be a high-stakes card game in the library after the concert. I had wandered in quite by accident looking for something to read. My attention was immediately captured by the ten or twelve people standing around in a corner.

As I joined the group, I realised they were watching a very intense game of three-card whist. Three men – none of whom I knew – were playing against the Baron, who was acting as the dealer. In the time that I was there, I saw the Baron win several hands, and there was some grumbling among the players while the spectators voiced their approval with each trick their host took.

As a result, I had precious little to report to Holmes when he entered my office disguised as a non-conformist clergyman on the Tuesday after my return. The only reason I recognised the minister as Holmes was because I had seen him don the exact same disguise on one or two previous occasions.

"So tell me, Watson, how was your weekend and what did you make of the Baron?"

"There is not much to tell, my friend. I spoke to Baron Leighton but once, and although there seemed to be other opportunities in which I might engage him in conversation, I followed your advice and refrained from initiating any conversation."

"Excellent, Watson. He is playing the long game here, and so must we. Other than that, how was your sojourn – not too taxing, I hope."

I then filled Holmes in about the people I had met and the various activities in which I had engaged. The only time he seemed genuinely interested was when I told him about the soprano.

"Yes, I have heard of her. I must make a point of it to attend one of her concerts. Anything else?"

I then related the story of the card game. When I had finished, Holmes remarked, "I had heard the Baron was quite adroit at cards. You don't think he was cheating, do you?"

"Honestly, I have no idea. With all those people looking on, I'm rather inclined to doubt it."

"It's the fact that all those people were watching which makes me think he might have been," Holmes replied.

"What on Earth do you mean?"

"Consider, Watson, for years audiences have watched John Maskelyne perform his levitation illusion, yet no one has ever detected exactly how it is done. Although they are looking carefully, they cannot divine the truth behind that simple bit of legerdemain."

"Simple?" I asked.

"Well, simple in the sense that we all know a woman cannot float in the air. However, when you consider the intricacies involved such as angles, costumes, lighting, background and the weight of the assistant, among other factors – not to mention the size of the apparatus – I suppose describing it as 'simple' is something of an injustice. Still, you see the point. It's an illusion, and cheating at cards is nothing more than another type of illusion – though not nearly so demanding."

"But why, Holmes? He appears to have plenty of money, and he seemingly wants for nothing."

"That is the question, Watson. When a man cheats, it says something about his character, and if a man is willing to swindle his friends at cards, who knows what else he might be capable of."

"So what's to be done? What is our next move?"

"At the moment we have no moves, old friend. I have examined all the evidence – paltry as it is – among the past deaths in which the Baron has been in close proximity. The trail is not cold; it is frozen tundra.

"So we seem to have reached an impasse, albeit a temporary one. For my part, I will continue to probe the Baron and his circle. At the same time, you must continue here in your practice. I think the rumors we discussed earlier may soon take root. Once they do, I should imagine you will be hearing from the Baron again. Also, I must apologise in advance for any distress they may cause you and Mrs. Watson."

"Hopefully, she will never hear of them, my friend. And if she should, well, that is a bridge I will cross when I come to it."

I bid Holmes good night, and having donned his disguise again, he left through the front just as he had entered.

Since Holmes and I were no longer "friends," I had to content myself with following his exploits in the daily papers. His name did not appear nearly so often as the intrepid Scotland Yard inspectors – Jones, Bradstreet, Gregson and, of course, Lestrade. However, knowing Holmes as I did, it was easy to see his hand in several high-profile cases.

One I remember vividly which occurred during our period of "estrangement" involved the death of Sir Franklin Conroy. Originally it was believed that Conroy, who had made his fortune as a tea grower in India, had succumbed to a heart attack. A bit of an eccentric, he was well-known among his social circle for placing ice in everything he drank – from the most dear single malt to the most aromatic teas. Apparently, he had never forgot nor forgiven the sweltering Indian clime in which he had dwelt for so long.

After he died, Holmes' investigation revealed someone had been mixing slivers of glass within Conroy's ice cubes. Although Lestrade was given credit for the arrest of the nephew who stood to profit handsomely from the inheritance, it was impossible not to discern Holmes as the prime mover in that little scenario.

To say that I missed my friend would be an understatement, but I also understood that I had a very specific role to play in the little drama he was orchestrating.

Some three weeks after Holmes had visited me in my surgery, I received a rather elaborate invitation in the morning post. The envelope, which appeared quite costly, had been sealed with red wax, and I recognised the imprint – a crown perched upon a knight's helm topped by two cog wheels – as Baron Leighton's.

Upon opening it, I learned that I had been invited to Brucastle Abbey two weeks hence for another of the Baron's weekend soirees. Since there was no way to contact Holmes at the moment, I decided to reply that I would be pleased to attend. I was certain that I would encounter Holmes within the next fortnight to make him aware of this latest development.

On the Wednesday night before I was to leave for the country, I was knackered after a grueling day at my surgery. To make matters worse, I was summoned to St. Barts where one of my patients had been admitted after being struck by a lorry. After examining his injuries – he apparently didn't trust the hospital physicians – I cleaned the deep gash in his skull and set his broken arm. Before I left, I suggested he stay overnight and come visit me the following week.

I took a cab home and the house was dark. I saw that it was nearly half ten, and I entered quietly so as not to wake Mary. I was stunned when I heard a familiar voice say, "Finally."

I turned to find Holmes sitting in my favourite chair, smiling at his own cleverness. "Were you responsible for Driscoll's accident?" I asked.

"Not at all. I came in through the back door just a few minutes after you had departed, and I've been waiting here ever since – without smoking, I might add."

"So then you know –"

"About your invitation, of course I do."

"Are my movements still being watched?"

"Indeed, they are. Otherwise, I would have used your front door and called upon you in a civilised manner. Now, there are several things I need you to do, but none more important than this." With that he reached inside his coat pocket and withdrew a sheaf of papers, and a small note book such as I often used when taking notes during one of our cases.

"What's this?"

"I need you to copy these pages," he said handing me the papers, "into this book. My prose style is certainly not on a par with your own, but these notes must be in your hand, and it is imperative you leave the notebook on the desk in your room at the abbey when you are out of your room."

"Do you think they are searching my room as well?"

"I have no doubt of it."

"What exactly are these notes?"

"Knowing your penchant for catchy titles – *A Study in Scarlet*, indeed! – I have set the groundwork for a story I have tentatively titled – 'The Case of the Deceptive Detective.'"

In spite of myself, I had to smile, "That's not half bad, you know. But what has the case to do with?"

"It's an exposé of sorts, in which you reveal you have grown tired of playing second-fiddle to me and putting up with my many," he paused for a second to consider his choice of words, then smiled and continued, "foibles, shall we say? Moreover, you confess that you often had more to do with the resolution of some cases than you might have led your readers to believe."

"The public will never accept that," I objected.

"This is not a story the public will ever see – it has only to appear to be one. Watson, people believe what they want to believe. You have always sold yourself short. Your powers of observation have improved dramatically since first we met."

"But Holmes, I can't read people like you do. Suppose someone asks me to do something like that."

"No one will ask – unless it is the Baron – and if he does, you merely explain such deductive chains are little more than a literary device you employ to make me appear far more intelligent than I am as well as to entice your readers to continue perusing the narrative."

"I wish I were as certain as you are."

"One more thing, Watson. After you have transcribed those pages, please burn them. If they should somehow fall into the wrong hands, all our planning and plotting will be for naught – and a murderer will walk free, presumably to kill again."

"I shall copy them tonight and make certain they are consumed by the fire as soon as I have finished."

"Excellent. Now, I will leave as I came."

As he reached the door, he stopped, looked back at me and said, "Thank you, old friend."

After he had departed, I poured myself a brandy, sat at my writing desk and began to copy the pages Holmes had left into the notebook.

I felt as though I were betraying my dearest friend as I began to write…

> *For too many years, I have helped perpetuate a fraud. I find that I can no longer live with that lie; as a result, I am determined to set the record straight.*
>
> *As my readers know, at our first meeting Sherlock Holmes greeted me with the words, "You have been in Afghanistan, I perceive."*

Truth be told, it was I who said to Holmes when we were introduced in the Criterion Bar, "You are not a physician, yet you work in the laboratory at St. Barts."

To say he was taken aback would be something of an understatement. He was totally nonplussed at my simple act of observation and deduction, and his next words to me were, "How on Earth could you have possibly known that?"

I continued writing for another two hours, and I must admit that I was impressed with the ease with which Holmes had been able to invert all the basic tenets of our relationship. As I plodded on, copying diligently, I remember thinking to myself, "If I didn't know either of the principals, this could certainly pass muster with me as a casual reader."

Then I was struck by the realization that anyone perusing these notes would be anything but a "casual reader" and that I had a certain role to play and there would be consequences if my performance were not convincing.

I spent another few hours transcribing and adding a few of my own editorial flourishes as I went along. I had to admit when I had finished that it was a pretty fair piece of fiction. I also had to concede Holmes was correct in his assessment: His prose style was certainly not on a par with my own.

By the time I had completed the transcription, the fire had died, but it quickly sprang to life when I added the fresh fuel. I watched as the flames licked the edges of the pages before consuming them greedily. After the flames had subsided, I stirred the ashes just to make certain there were no telltale remnants of paper left.

Satisfied, I headed for my bed, and as I was undressing I realised that I was actually looking forward to my weekend and testing myself in a situation that seemed fraught with peril.

Chapter 8

On Friday afternoon, I caught the 3:04 from King's Cross. This time I rode alone in my first-class compartment. I enjoyed the solitude and was able to read quite a bit of Wilkie Collins' *The Woman in White*. I was quite taken with the manner in which he kept switching narrators. It was quite different from what I had done in *A Study in Scarlet*, and I was wondering if I might be able to do something similar in one of my Holmes stories.

At any rate, I was so engrossed in the tale that before I knew it, the conductor was announcing, "Brucastle Abbey." I had a different driver and rode to the abbey alone. Once there, I was shown to the same room. While I was unpacking, one of the servants knocked on the door and informed me, "Refreshments are presently being served in the library. Dinner will be served at eight o'clock."

Since I had not eaten lunch, I decided to see what was transpiring in the library. It also would afford me the opportunity to see if I knew anyone else.

There were several platters of cold meats and cheeses as well as assorted wines and something stronger for those who wished it. There was also a big bowl of punch that I am certain featured spirits of some sort. As I was enjoying a glass of very fine chardonnay, a woman approached me. "Excuse me," she said, "but are you Dr. John Watson?"

"I am."

"*The* Dr. Watson who writes those wonderful stories about Mr. Sherlock Holmes?"

"I am he," I replied, "and while I don't know how wonderful my stories are, I am rather glad that you enjoy them."

Taking stock of her now, I realised that she was older than I had initially thought, but she was still an attractive woman, svelte and with a certain regal bearing that those less gifted by nature might find off-putting; however, I found her confidence attractive.

Unfortunately, her remarks had been overheard by others nearby, and I suddenly discovered I was the centre of attention of a small group of people – all of whom wanted to know more about Holmes.

I spent some time answering questions and – though it upset me terribly – occasionally depicting my friend in a less than favourable light. When the novelty of my presence had worn off, I turned to get another glass of wine and found myself face to face with the rather formidable presence of Baron Friedrich Leighton. A stout man, perhaps a bit shorter than I, the Baron boasted a sturdy frame and possessed the greenest eyes I have I ever seen. In a deep bass voice, he said, "Dr. Watson, so good to see you again." Still smiling, he continued, "I can see you are tired of talking about Mr. Holmes, but one more question, if you would indulge me?"

"Certainly," I replied, "and thank you for inviting me again."

The Baron waved away my compliment and said, "Think nothing of it. I am rather hoping you will become a regular at my little get-togethers. Now, and please pardon my directness, I have formed the distinct impression that you don't care all that much for Mr. Holmes."

I must admit the man's frankness took me aback. After a few seconds, I replied, "Holmes is a man of many talents and great intelligence, but his eccentricities can be a bit trying at times."

"Well-played, Doctor! Still I must confess that I believe if you were to be totally candid, there is more about Mr. Holmes than his 'eccentricities' that annoy you."

I was about to ask "What gives you that impression?" when two women and a man came up to us. One of the women said, "Freddy, we are hoping to play a rubber or two of whist before dinner, and we need a fourth."

The Baron looked at me, shrugged, turned to the trio and said, "Usual stakes?" As he left, he took two steps, looked back over his shoulder at me and said, "I do hope we can continue this conversation later – perhaps over an after-dinner drink."

I could only nod and say, "It would be my pleasure."

A few hours later we all enjoyed a delightful meal, the main course of which featured roasted goose as well as trout almondine with roasted root vegetables. I noticed the Baron, who had left during the middle of the meal, had yet to return. As the waiters were pouring coffee and serving cordials, one of them approached me and said softly, "The Baron would like you to join him in his study."

I followed the young man, and a few minutes later entered the study. The waiter said to me, "The Baron will be with you shortly."

Left to my own devices, I took stock of my surroundings and couldn't help but notice what a handsome room it was. Three of the walls featured bookshelves from floor to ceiling – all of which were filled with handsomely bound volumes. The fourth wall was almost entirely windows,

One of the other three, featured an oversize fireplace with bookshelves on either side. The wall opposite the windows was broken up by two portraits – presumably some ancestors of the Baron – hanging high on the wall above a sidebar laden with an assortment of bottles and glasses. In between the sidebar and the portraits was the family crest which featured four quadrants of red and gold with a single-arched bridge spanning the shield. At the top was a crown perched upon a knight's helm topped by two cog wheels. I thought it most unusual and was planning to ask the Baron about it. The last wall contained the only door, which again was bracketed by bookshelves. All in all, it was a most inviting room.

On the wall with the windows overlooking the gardens, two overstuffed chairs had been placed in front of an enormous desk of glistening dark wood. Behind the desk was an even more ornate chair of luxurious brown leather, its back to the windows.

I began by inspecting the room more closely – not quite certain exactly what I was expecting to find. Upon looking closer, I realised the portraits were considerably older than I had at first imagined. I have already commented on the fully stocked sidebar. The fireplace struck me as unusual, because it was brickwork encased in a wooden frame. The wood appeared to be mahogany and was obviously well-cared for. The fire grate made me chuckle for it featured two wolves rampant, their paws placed on a large cauldron. I had never seen anything quite like it before.

I then began to inspect the books. I cannot be certain, but one of the tomes that caught my eye – perhaps because it had been given pride of place in the centre shelf – was a bound volume of Shakespeare's works that I thought might be a clever facsimile of the First Folio. I was weighing whether I should examine the book more closely when a voice behind me suddenly said, "It's genuine, Dr. Watson. Feel free to examine it if you like. In fact, feel free to borrow it or anything else in the library that strikes your fancy."

I turned to see Baron Leighton standing, perhaps ten feet away. I hadn't heard him enter the room, but then I had been thoroughly engrossed in my examination of the library's holdings.

"I wouldn't dream of such a thing," I managed.

"Well, the offer stands." Then he laughed and said, "Where are my manners? Let me begin by thanking you, Dr. Watson, for joining me. I've been hoping that we could talk for some time now, but my schedule has been rather unrelenting of late."

"Not at all. It is I who should be thanking you. Your hospitality apparently knows no bounds."

"Speaking of hospitality, may I offer you a drink – brandy? A cordial? Perhaps you would enjoy a glass of this single malt I have been saving for a special occasion."

"I rather doubt that I could ever be considered a special occasion by anyone other than my wife."

"Then let's drink to her, shall we?"

I could hardly refuse such a chivalrous offer, and I've always enjoyed a fine single malt.

As the Baron walked towards the sidebar, I noticed he had an almost imperceptible limp. Selecting a dark green bottle, the Baron explained, "This is Laphroaig. It is distilled in the Islay section of Scotland from waters provided by the Kilbride Dam. It is quite smoky on the nose and has a pronounced peaty flavor on the palate. It's not to everyone's taste, but I've developed an appreciation for it – especially in the cooler months."

He then poured two small snifters, filling them a third of the way with a liquid that was gold with a slightly reddish hue. "You must savor the aroma before you taste it," he explained.

Then he looked at me and smiled, raised his glass and said, "To Mrs. Watson, your muse!"

We clinked glasses and I took a sip of one of the finest single malts I had ever tasted.

The Baron said, "You like it. I can tell."

"Indeed, I do," I replied.

"Excellent! So tell me, are you enjoying yourself here Dr. Watson?" he asked gesturing me to a chair.

"Very much so," I replied, and then the Baron, who had taken the seat opposite mine, and I proceeded to discuss various and sundry topics. It was almost as though I were chatting with Holmes, so I had to keep reminding myself that the man sitting across from me, chatting amiably, might well be a highly paid killer. I am well aware that my face is an open book – Holmes having told me as much on numerous occasions – so I was not unduly surprised when the Baron suddenly asked, "Is there something wrong, Doctor?"

"Nothing, nothing at all. I fear that I've taken up too much of your time. After all, you do have other guests."

"Nonsense," he replied as he freshened my drink. "I so seldom meet anyone who is truly interesting, so when I do, I take full advantage of the opportunity."

And so we continued talking, smoking and drinking. I must confess the Baron was far more adept at holding his liquor than I, and I could tell my words were starting to slur – and that must have been right before I nodded off.

Sometime later I awoke with a pounding headache matched only by the equally loud pounding on the door. I looked around and was stunned to discover that it was morning. I was alone in the room and assumed that the Baron had just let me sleep it off in the chair while he went to bed.

Stretching, for I was stiff and painful, having spent hours in the same position. I yelled at the door, "Just a moment."

I went to the door, turned the knob and was stunned to discover that it was locked. "There's no key in the lock," I yelled.

The voice on the other side replied, "The Baron always keeps an extra key in the top right drawer of his desk."

As I made my way to the desk, I wondered why the Baron had locked me in the library. As I reached the desk, I saw the Baron was sitting in his chair, facing away from me, looking out the windows. "You too, Lord Leighton? They were ready to knock down the door, shall I try to hold them off for a few minutes?"

When I received no answer, I walked around the chair to face the Baron and that was when I saw the bloodstains on his shirt and realized the Baron wasn't sleeping; he was dead.

Chapter 9

Words cannot convey the whirlwind of emotions that consumed me at that moment. I was stunned, confused, angry and frightened all at once. Briefly, I thought about trying to escape through the window, but I realised that would only make me appear guilty.

"Dr. Watson, will you please open the door. I have an important message for the Baron."

Thinking quickly, I replied, "The Baron is indisposed, and I am treating him. Kindly slip it under the door."

As an envelope appeared under the door, a thought hit me. "The Baron would like you to wire Sherlock Holmes at 221B Baker Street in London and inform him his presence is required here immediately. Tell him it is most urgent, and he should bring Inspector Lestrade with him as well."

I was uncertain what to do next. I took the envelope and placed it on the Baron's desk – and then it hit me: With every step, I was disturbing the crime scene. I considered leaving the room, but then I realised someone had been in what appeared to be a locked room and that person had departed without leaving a trace.

Fearing that if I did exit the room, the culprit might return and wreak more mayhem, I returned to my chair and sat as still as possible.

The sun was high in the afternoon sky, and I was ravenously hungry when I finally heard a knock on the door, followed by my friend's voice through the door. "Watson, are you in there?"

"Yes, Holmes. Just give me a moment to open the door." Using the key I had found in the desk, I admitted Holmes and

Lestrade and quickly closed the door behind them, locking it after they had entered.

I then proceeded to tell Holmes and Lestrade everything that had happened to the best of my ability, concluding with, "So I remained here all day knowing you would want the crime scene as undisturbed as possible."

"You have done well, my friend."

"You may believe that, Mr. Holmes," said Lestrade, "but things aren't looking too good for the Doctor here." At that point, Lestrade went to the door and informed the butler of the Baron's death. He then instructed the man to send for the local police as well as a clergyman, if appropriate.

"Lestrade, you can't be serious," I exclaimed. "After all, I am the one who summoned Holmes and yourself."

"It wouldn't be the first time a killer called the police," replied Lestrade.

As we continued to bicker, Holmes set about examining the room. As he stood by the body of the Baron, I noticed again that his shirt was stained with blood. I had seen the blood when I first realized the Baron had been slain. However, I hadn't realized just how much blood he had lost. I can only attribute my oversight to the after-effects of the whisky.

We stood and watched as Holmes examined the body, the desk, the sidebar and the door. He even knocked on the walls, presumably looking for a secret passage of some sort – but to no avail. Finally, he sat in the chair, where the Baron had sat the previous evening, steepled his fingers, stretched out his long legs, and closed his eyes. I had seen him adopt this pose many times and knew that he was deep in thought. After a few minutes, Lestrade made as though to speak, but I looked at him and shook my head no. Surprisingly, Lestrade heeded my warning, so for several more minutes we watched in absolute silence as Holmes puzzled things out in his mind.

I could see Lestrade's patience had worn thin, and he was just getting ready to speak when Holmes finally said, "Lestrade, would you be so kind as to lay out the case against Dr. Watson?"

The inspector began to speak, "Dr. Watson was found in a locked room with the deceased; since there is only one door and the windows appear to have remained bolted, it stands to reason that Doctor Watson is our prime suspect."

After a pause, he continued, "I suppose he could have opened the windows and let someone in who killed Baron Leighton, but that would still make him an accessory to murder."

Holmes smiled, "And how was the Baron killed?"

"He appears to have been stabbed to death."

"Excellent, Lestrade. And where is the murder weapon?"

"It must be hidden somewhere in this room."

"You may search all you like," Holmes said, "but I fear you will never find it. Also, given the copious amount of blood on the Baron's shirt and dinner jacket, I am inclined to think that the attacker would also bear some evidence of blood on his clothing, yet if you look, you will see that Watson's shirt is as white as snow – albeit a bit more wrinkled."

"He could have stabbed him from behind, or he could have let someone in as I said," Lestrade countered.

"Then his sleeve would be bloodstained, and that is not the case, Moreover, if the Baron were attacked from behind, the wounds would have been inflicted with downward thrusts, and a close examination will show that the wounds all are level or slightly upward – indicating the attacker was, if not the same height as the Baron, perhaps an inch or two shorter. You will notice that Watson is at least an inch, possibly two, taller than the Baron.

"As for letting someone in, those windows have not been opened for several days. There are no tracks anywhere – and finally, what would Watson's motive be?

"No, Lestrade, it simply will not do. I grant you a superficial examination might lead one to suspect Watson initially, but those premises would fall apart almost immediately upon closer inspection."

"But Mr. Holmes, Doctor Watson was the only one here. No one else could have got in or out, you just said so. You've tested the walls. Did any of them sound hollow?"

"I must admit the answer is no."

"Well then…" replied Lestrade, letting his words trail off.

"Lestrade, you have known Watson, what is it now eight years? Do you think he is capable of such a crime?"

"Under normal circumstances, absolutely not – but who's to say what a man is capable of when he's well into his cups as Doctor Watson admittedly was."

"I have a maxim," Holmes said, "I know Watson is familiar with it. When you have eliminated the impossible, whatever remains, however improbable, must be the solution."

I had to smile in spite of myself as Lestrade asked, "What exactly does that mean?"

"I mean Watson didn't kill the Baron, so someone else did."

Lestrade started to say, "But that's imposs—" when he saw Holmes smiling at him. Stopping himself, the inspector continued, "I see your point, Mr. Holmes."

"So where are we gentlemen? First, let's return to the scene. Watson, what was your beverage of choice last evening?"

"We were drinking a single malt, Laphroaig."

"I am familiar with it. And you were seated here?" Holmes inquired pointing to my chair. I nodded. "And the Baron here?" he said indicating the other chair. I nodded again. "Presumably those are your glasses here on this table?"

"Yes," I replied.

Holmes then examined the tumblers. They were heavy, made from cut crystal, perhaps Waterford. "Interesting," he said. "Very interesting."

"What might that be?" asked Lestrade.

"Notice Inspector, the inside of Watson's glass is perfectly dry while the Baron's contains small traces of the scotch. We could discuss the various properties of liquids such as adhesion and cohesion, but I hope you will trust me when I say this is not Watson's glass – but a substitute."

"But why?" I exclaimed.

"I believe you were drugged last night, Watson. Perhaps laudanum, the taste of which was masked by the scotch. I believe that Laphroaig has a rather distinctive peaty aroma and flavor – perfect for concealing the presence of a drug."

I could only nod and say, "You have it exactly."

Holmes had been looking about the room while we were talking. Finally Lestrade said, "Pray tell, Mr. Holmes, what exactly is it you're looking for?"

"The bottle of Laphroaig, which I've just found." Picking up the bottle from the sideboard carefully with a handkerchief, Holmes showed us the bottle and asked, "Is this what you were drinking?"

"Indeed," I replied. "Though I could go quite some time without tasting it again."

"Consider, Lestrade. There are no fingerprints that I can discern, and it's only about one-third gone."

"We drank far more than that," I said red-facedly.

"Yes, I imagine you did," said Holmes wryly.

"That's all fine and dandy, but it proves nothing. It's all circumstantial. I am afraid I must take Dr. Watson into custody. I'm certain you'll be able to prove his innocence, but I must do my job. I have my superiors to answer to."

"Lestrade, I have eliminated the impossible – that Dr. Watson killed the Baron. All that remains is to consider the improbable – that someone else added the laudanum to the Scotch – although I am inclined to think that was the Baron's handiwork."

"But why?" I asked.

"The 'why' can be dealt with later. At the moment, let us focus on the problem at hand – the 'how.'"

Suddenly, there was a knock at the door. "Inspector Lestrade, the parish priest is here to offer prayers for the repose of the soul of the Baron. The local police are on their way."

I looked at Holmes and saw the beginning of a faint smile starting to play across his face.

"Do show him in, Lestrade," replied Holmes. "I have a theory that will want testing. A few minutes later, the Rev. Thomas Grinbe entered the room. He looked around as if uncertain to whom he should offer his condolences.

Finally, Lestrade spoke up, "We are not relatives, Father. I am Inspector Lestrade of Scotland Yard and these gentlemen are Mr. Sherlock Holmes and Dr., John Watson."

After acknowledging us, the priest inquired, "Will you allow me to pray for the deceased?"

"Of course," said Lestrade.

We watched as the clergyman donned a stole, blessed himself and then the body and then began to pray quietly. When he had finished, he thanked us and said the undertaker would be along presently. As he started to leave, Holmes said, "Father, a word?"

"Of course, Mr. Holmes," replied the priest.

"You are a recent convert to Catholicism, are you not?"

"I am," he replied, "but how could you possibly know that?"

"Your Latin pronunciation leaves a bit to be desired, and the obvious care you employed during the ritual of blessing the Baron all suggest a man who has only recently adopted the Roman Catholic faith as his own. You were a member of the High Anglican Church, I believe," and when the priest nodded, Holmes continued, "Perhaps we can discuss your conversion further at another time.

"May I ask to which order you belong?"

"I am a member of the Dominicans. The order was founded by St. Dominic in Toulouse, France, in 1216."

"I was rather hoping you might be a Jesuit," replied Holmes.

The priest looked puzzled, but Holmes continued undeterred, "May I ask you a few more questions, Father?"

The priest continued looking confused but responded, "Of course, Mr. Holmes."

With that they withdrew to the other side of the room and stood by the fireplace. Holmes and the priest were soon engrossed in conversation. Lestrade and I could do nothing but watch. At one point, I saw Holmes point to the floor, the priest looked down, then crouched in front of the fireplace, looked up at Holmes and nodded in the affirmative.

Holmes then walked with the priest to the door and said, "Thank you, Father. Your assistance has proved invaluable."

With that the rather nonplussed clergyman bid us good day and left the room. No sooner had he departed than Lestrade asked, "What was all that about, Mr. Holmes?"

"I was merely testing a theory, Inspector." Pointing to the framed paintings on the wall, he said, "Tell me what you see, Lestrade."

"There are two portraits, presumably some ancestors of the Baron's, I would think."

"And?"

"A coat of arms; again, I presume that is the Baron's heraldic crest."

"It is, indeed," said Holmes, "you can see the family motto – *per veritatem et diligentiam* – 'By Truth and Diligence' – inscribed there on the banderole across the bottom."

"What of it?"

"Would you agree that, given the presence of the coat of arms and the portraits, the Baron took some degree of pride in his forebears?"

"That seems logical," replied Lestrade.

"So then tell me, Inspector, why would a man proud of his family and his title have the coat of arms of another family displayed rather prominently in the same room?"

Lestrade and I both looked around searching for another coat of arms. When the inspector finally looked at me, and I shook my head, I could see that he was as perplexed as I. At last he gave voice to his frustration and said, "Mr. Holmes, I have seen you do these sorts of things for years. Must I remind you that we are talking about murder here, and right now Dr. Watson is our chief suspect? I do hope that priests and portraits and coats of arms have some small bearing on this case. Otherwise, much as it pains me, I am going to have place Dr. Watson under arrest and you can visit him at the Yard."

Chapter 10

"If you would be kind enough to do me a small favour, Lestrade. I would like you and Watson to go outside in the hall for exactly two minutes and then re-enter the room."

"And what will you be doing?" asked Lestrade. "Not tinkering with evidence, I hope."

"I think you know me better than that, Inspector, so I beg you to indulge me."

"And then as soon as the local constabulary arrives, we can be on our way?"

"You have my word, Inspector."

With that Lestrade and I went into the hall and locked the door behind us. The last I saw of Holmes, he was sitting in the chair I had used and smoking a cigarette.

After two minutes exactly, we re-entered the room and were stunned to discover it was empty. Holmes was nowhere to be seen. Lestrade examined the windows which were still locked, then he began to knock on the walls as Holmes had done. When he had finished, he looked at me, but all I could do was shrug. Finally in frustration, Lestrade bellowed, "Where are you Holmes? What kind of trick is this?"

To which a voice from behind us replied evenly, "I am right here, Inspector, No need to yell."

"But how? Where were you hiding? How did you do it?"

"The same way the person who killed the Baron did it?"

Red-faced, Lestrade seethed, "Now, I know there's a hiding place – but where is it? I searched this room."

"As did I," replied Holmes, "and, truth be told, I missed it on my first examination as well."

"Holmes, please explain yourself," I asked.

Looking at us, he said, "Have you ever heard of a priest hole?"

"Can't say that I have," replied Lestrade. "I'm a Presbyterian myself – never had much to do with the Papists."

I shook my head no as well.

"I thought as much," said Holmes, "Please allow me to enlighten you. As I am sure you are aware, during the reign of Queen Elizabeth, Catholics were persecuted and in some instances put to death. Despite the fines and threats, many nobles remained loyal to the pope, and they had secret services conducted in their homes.

"As the persecution increased, a number of them built secret compartments in their homes for the priests to hide in, should the house suddenly be searched. Many of the priest holes were constructed by one Nicholas Owen, a lay Jesuit brother, at the end of the sixteenth and beginning of the seventeenth centuries. For more than two decades, he constructed priest holes in some of the kingdom's finest residences."

"Obviously, there is a priest hole in this room," replied Lestrade, who had regained control of his emotions. "Now where the devil is it?"

With that Holmes went to the fireplace and bent over the fire gate for a second, and suddenly pulled it up – perhaps an inch or two. As he did so, the back of the fireplace slid in perhaps a foot or two, revealing a small passage,"

"Well I'll be," said Lestrade. "Where does it lead?"

"There's a flight of steps at the end of the passage that leads to the wine cellar. The door below has been concealed in a large cask."

"How on Earth did you ever come to suspect its location?"

"I was struck by the design of the fire gate. It reminded me of something but I couldn't quite put my figure on it. When the priest arrived, it triggered the memory."

"What memory?" I asked.

"I once had occasion to visit Harvington Hall in Worcestershire. The local magistrate gave me a tour of the estate showing me the various hides scattered throughout the house, one of which had been cleverly concealed in a fireplace. In that one, the priest would enter and then climb a ladder taking him to a much larger refuge concealed in the garret."

"But what made you suspect there was one here?"

"The fire gate."

"The fire gate?" sputtered Lestrade.

"Yes," replied Holmes. "The one at Harvington Hall is identical to the one here in this room."

"But how is that possible? And what of the second coat of arms you spoke of?" I asked.

"If you look at the gate, you will notice two wolves with their paws resting on a cauldron. The Spanish words for wolf and cauldron are *lobo* and *olla* respectively, and when you combine them, you get …"

"Loyola," I exclaimed. "No doubt referring to St. Ignatius Loyola, founder of the Society of Jesus, also known as the Jesuits. So that was why you asked the priest about his order."

"Splendid, Watson. You are in top form today, despite your rough night. The Jesuits were a particular annoyance to Queen Elizabeth as the order kept dispatching missionaries to England. They may also have played no small role in convincing King Philip to deploy the Spanish Armada against her. When I finally remembered where I had seen a similar gate, everything fell into place."

"So what was the point of all this?" asked Lestrade.

"Obviously to incriminate Doctor Watson, and perhaps in some way be avenged against me."

"But why was the Baron killed?" asked Lestrade.

"I think the Baron was deceived and felt he would play a role in having Watson arrested. I'm certain he had no idea what that role would be. Purely as a matter of conjecture, I think the Baron had become a liability. He was attracting attention, and that's something most criminals studiously avoid."

"So what do we do next?" I asked.

"We begin by determining who actually killed the Baron. Given what we know – as well as what we suspect – about the man, I have no doubt that will prove a daunting task."

As he spoke, I noticed the gleam in his eye. This was Holmes at his best – marshalling all his resources and bringing them to bear on a case which he deemed worthy of his talents.

"Lestrade, I will now examine the passageway in greater detail; however, I am not optimistic. Whoever carried this out was quite organised and meticulous in their planning. Were it not for the clean glass, they might have got away with it."

With that, he turned and disappeared into the priest hole, leaving Lestrade and me to look at each other perplexedly. "Well, he certainly saved your bacon, Dr. Watson."

"Indeed," I replied. I was tempted to add a snarky remark along the lines of, "No thanks to you," but I refrained.

"I'm going to interview the staff and some of the other guests." As he reached the door, Lestrade turned back to me and said, "No hard feelings, I hope, Doctor. I was merely doing my job."

"I understand, Inspector," I replied, and I was glad I had held my tongue.

After he had departed, I walked to the fireplace and called out, "Holmes?"

"Coming, Watson," he answered, and a moment later he emerged.

"Have you learned anything?"

"Only that we are facing a most formidable foe," he replied with just a hint of excitement in his voice.

"Holmes, I want to thank you."

"Think nothing of it," he replied. "It is I who should be thanking you for bringing an extra layer of obfuscation to a case that had already presented a serious challenge."

"What on Earth do you mean?"

"I think we – and I include myself, you, Lestrade and the Baron in this scenario – have all been manipulated. I think we were deliberately set upon the Baron's scent, and I followed it dutifully. You remember the note in the dead man's pocket with our address?"

"Yes," I replied. "What of it?"

"If you recall, it was printed in block letters. Since we were not yet formally involved and I knew nothing of the victim, it didn't strike me as unusual. Now, I am more inclined to think the note was planted there for Lestrade to find and thus seek my help."

"To what end?"

"That remains to be determined. Although they have left no discernable clues, whoever is behind this has made one critical error."

"And what would that be?"

"They have made it personal." With that he turned toward the door and said, "If we hurry Watson, we can catch the evening train back to London."

I could only marvel at Holmes' ability to approach a problem so methodically.

"Just let me pack, and we can be on our way."

A few minutes later we bade farewell to Lestrade, who promised to explain my role in this sordid affair to the locals. I guaranteed that I would make myself available should they have any pressing questions. The last I saw of the good inspector that day he was still waiting impatiently for the local lawmen to arrive. On our way to the station, we passed what could only be the undertaker's wagon, which was followed closely by another carriage in which sat two stolid, stern looking men who could only be members of the local constabulary.

At that moment, I was very glad to leave Brucastle Abbey behind.

Chapter 11

The train ride home was spent in silence. I could see the gears in Holmes' head turning as he tried to construct a thesis. I knew he had precious little data with which to work, so I remained silent and watched the countryside pass. I must admit that I, too, was trying to figure out the "who" and the "why" behind the attempt to have me imprisoned or at best incommoded.

As we disembarked at King's Cross station, Holmes finally broke the silence, "Might I suggest you accompany me to Baker Street? We have a great deal to discuss."

I readily agreed, and at that point I began to realise how exceedingly hungry I was. Holmes generally eschewed food when he was involved with a case, but I am not made of nearly such stern stuff. Fortunately, Mrs. Hudson had made a stew that evening and there was plenty left for the two of us.

After eating, we sat in our chairs before the fire and enjoyed a brandy and cigars. Finally, Holmes spoke, "I am certain you recall at the conclusion of the affair that you so reprehensibly titled *The Valley of Fear*, I mentioned a man named Moriarty?"

"Indeed, I believe your exact words were, 'I can tell a Moriarty when I see one.'"

"Just so," he replied. "I believe this attempt to have you arrested for the murder of Baron Leighton is also a Moriarty."

"Do you believe that fellow was at Brucastle Abbey?"

"No, no, not at all. Moriarty would never soil his hands so. However, I should hate to be the underling who so badly botched this that you were allowed to walk free – let alone escape a night in gaol."

At that moment, there was a knock on the door. "Do come in, Mrs. Hudson," Holmes said.

"I meant to give this to you as soon as you arrived, but with Dr. Watson being so hungry, it slipped my mind while I was preparing your dinner." With that, she handed Holmes an envelope.

He glanced at it, but before reading it, he asked, "When did this arrive?"

"Not ten minutes after you left this morning. It came in the third morning post." After saying that, she curtseyed and left.

Holmes then opened the envelope and read it. "It is as I feared." He then handed me the letter. There were but three lines, which read:

> *Revenge is a dish best served cold*
> *– and in several courses.*
> *Dear me, Mr. Holmes! Dear me!*

"And there you have it," my friend said, "Proof, if it were needed, that Moriarty is behind this entire thing. The fact that I was supposed to get this message this morning is most interesting."

"How so?"

"He obviously counted on his plan succeeding, else why gloat like this?"

"So what's to be done?"

"The first thing I must insist upon is that your wife pay that long, overdue visit to her relatives in Wales as soon as possible."

"She has no relatives in Wales," I protested.

"Perhaps you are not familiar with that branch of the Morstan family tree. I know you will feel better once she is safe, and I am going to need you at your best as we try to bring these blackguards to justice. You need not concern yourself with the particulars of her trip, just explain to her that her safety is paramount and that's why these extraordinary measures must be taken."

"But for how long?" I asked.

"That remains to be seen. Unfortunately, that is something that is beyond our control," he replied.

I saw his point immediately and said, "I will do whatever must be done."

"Then I would suggest while she is away, you move back in here with me. It will be easier to strategise and plan, and you know I find you invaluable as a sounding board."

I agreed with everything Holmes had said. As I prepared to leave for my home, I was dreading having to explain everything to Mary. As I reached the door, Holmes said, "There will be a cab outside your home tomorrow morning at eight o'clock exactly. Follow the driver's instructions to the letter, and I will see you here sometime in the afternoon or early evening."

Fortunately, Mary was far more understanding than I had any right to expect her to be. After I had finished explaining everything, omitting a few parts so as to spare her needless worry, she simply said, "I knew you and Mr. Holmes were up to something."

"And how did you know that?"

She laughed, "I told you – the new suits, the dinner jacket, two weekends away. It's a simple matter of deduction, really."

I laughed in spite of myself and reflected again upon my good fortune at meeting and wedding this remarkable woman.

The next morning we packed our bags and as promised, the hansom was waiting for us. As we alighted at King's Cross station, the driver handed me an envelope with our tickets inside and we soon boarded a train for Cardiff. We had a first-class compartment to ourselves until a middle-aged man joined us.

Before I could say it was a private compartment, he said in a broad Scots burr, "Dr. Watson, my name is Craig Campbell. I've been asked by Mr. Holmes to keep an eye on you and Mrs. Watson. Your tickets say Cardiff, but we'll be getting off at Reading."

"How do I know you are from Holmes?"

With that he handed me an envelope. I recognised Holmes' spidery scrawl at once. The note simply said: *"You can trust Campbell. S.H."*

So as not to bore you with the details, let me just say that Mrs. Watson continued on to Wales with Mr. Campbell while I traveled cross-country and caught another train that returned me to London.

As I entered our sitting room late that afternoon, Holmes turned to me and said, "You'll be happy to know that your wife has arrived in Swansea – albeit by a most circuitous route – and she will be well cared for. Campbell is quite a dependable man."

I expressed my gratitude and then inquired, "Have you made any progress?"

"Not much I am afraid. Although I am certain Moriarty is involved, there is something about this that feels intensely personal. The animosity is almost palpable. I am beginning to think we are dealing with someone who feels I have badly wronged him or her, and that person is working in concert with Moriarty. I spent last evening reviewing past cases, and I must say, I have made a fair number of enemies."

I had to smile at Holmes' modesty, never one of his strengths. Without giving it much thought, I began to tick off names, "Let's see, for starters, you might consider John Clay and Culverton Smith. Of more recent vintage, we have Jonas Oldacre, the Beddington brothers and let us not forget Jephro Rucastle."

"They are all in prison, dead or otherwise accounted for."

"One of them might have hired an agent of some sort."

"Most certainly an agent has been employed, but I am inclined to think there is much more to this than meets the eye. Remember the note seems to suggest several efforts will be made against me.

"I think you are on the right track, old friend, but I think we must cast a broader net. Now, you must be famished. Mrs. Hudson has prepared something special for your return. So let us eat and then we will talk some more."

After our meal of savory pork, one of my favourites, we adjourned to our chairs and were enjoying Port and cigars, when I asked Holmes, "What did you mean by casting a wider net?"

"It's obvious none of the men you named could move against me personally, which brings us then to family and other close associates. Does John Clay have a brother? An uncle? An unknown partner? Do any of those men? That is what we must determine?"

"Holmes, there are three million souls in this city. How will you possibly locate the individual in question?"

"Given what transpired at Brucastle Abbey, I am certain that the perpetrator will seek me out. So I must be ready for attacks from all sides. I have already requested the visitor logs from Pentonville Prison and the other facilities where the various men are incarcerated."

"In the meantime, I will continue to peruse my year books and carry on with my daily routines."

It was such an innocent pronouncement, and yet at the time, I had no idea of the maelstrom that awaited us.

Three days later, there was a pounding at the door shortly after breakfast. I heard Mrs. Hudson open the door and then she cautioned, "Wait a minute! You can't go up there." Obviously, our visitor had ignored her protestations because seconds later there was a pounding on our door, and I heard a boy's voice yelling, "Mr. 'Olmes! Mr. 'Olmes! We need your 'elp!"

My friend beat me to the door and when he opened it, a youngster no more than ten or eleven stood there with his cap in his hands. Although I didn't know his name, I did recognise him as one of Holmes' street Arabs – a member of the group he referred to as the Baker Street Irregulars.

"Timmins, what on Earth is wrong?"

"The coppers, Mr. 'Olmes. They pinched Wiggins."

"Are you saying Wiggins has been arrested?"

I was stunned. Wiggins was the leader of the Irregulars and although he may have engaged in a few shady practices in the past, since he had been in Holmes' employ, he had walked the straight and narrow as far as I knew.

"Arrested? Where? And on what charge?" asked Holmes.

"They nicked 'im by the Portobello Market where 'is family owns a stall."

"What is he accused of?"

"The coppers said 'e was selling stolen goods. They searched 'is family's stall and found some wallets and watches belonging to a bunch of toffs. They said Wiggins stole 'em to sell 'em. As they was takin' 'im away, 'e told me to find you and tell you what 'ad 'appened."

"Do you happen to know the arresting officer?"

"Yes, sir, 'is name is Jones – 'e 'as a real funny first name."

"That would be Athelney Jones," said Holmes.

"That's the bloke," exclaimed the lad.

"Timmins, go outside and hail a cab. We shall be down directly."

After donning coats and hats, for the weather had turned cooler, we were soon in a hansom headed for the Kensington police station. Perhaps twenty minutes later, we found ourselves sitting across the desk from Inspector Athelney Jones. I had first met Jones the previous year when he was involved with investigating the murder of Bartholomew Sholto in a case I had titled *The Sign of Four*. It was also the case where I had met my wife.

"Always a pleasure to see you, Mr. Holmes, and you as well, Dr. Watson," the policeman said amiably. "I know why you're here, but I'm afraid there is little you can do to help the lad. We found the goods hidden in a box in the back of the family stall."

"Pray tell, Inspector, what exactly was in the box?"

"Here, you may see for yourself," he replied reaching down to the floor and lifting up a wooden fruit crate which he placed in the center of his desk."

Holmes then began to examine the various items in the box which contained several pocket watches, two wristwatches, a few different fountain pens and perhaps ten or twelve wallets and billfolds of various styles.

Holmes then took out his lens and re-examined the watches, taking notes on his cuff as he often did. I can only assume he was looking for inscriptions and other possible clues. After he had finished with the watches, he turned to the wallets – all of which contained a number of notes of varying denominations. When he had finished, he said to Jones, "Don't you think it odd, the notes were left in the wallets?"

I could see that Jones was taken aback by the question, but he answered, "Nothing the criminal mind does surprises me anymore, Mr. Holmes."

"True, true," replied Holmes, "yet one must wonder why the lad accumulated so much without disposing of any of it. Normally, thieves steal and then unload their ill-gotten gains as quickly as possible at the nearest pawnshop."

"It does give one pause, now that you mention it," replied Jones. "Perhaps he's just a young thief, still learning the ropes."

"Might I ask how you came to suspect young Wiggins of these crimes?"

"We received a letter saying it would be in the public's interest to check out the stall on Portobello where one Wiggins is employed."

"I don't suppose you have the letter?" asked Holmes.

"Of course I do," replied Jones in a tone that suggested he was offended by Holmes' implied suggestion that his files might be anything but fastidious.

After looking in one of his desk drawers, he handed a slip of paper to Holmes. "It's just as I suspected," said my friend. Showing me the missive, he said, "The cheapest paper possible and a message scrawled in pencil in a hand that is almost indecipherable. This tells us nothing."

"What's that you say, Mr. Holmes?"

"Inspector, you have known me for several years now."

"Indeed, and you have helped me on a fair number of occasions."

"Then I trust you will believe me when I say that young Wiggins is the innocent victim of a plot against me. I have offered you some suggestions that would seem to indicate he is guiltless of the charges. What I would you like you to do is keep Wiggins here and treat him well. It must appear as though he has been charged and will stand trial. You may even let it about that you hope to see him end up in a reformatory school. Tell no one else except Lestrade about this plan, but it is most important that the lad remain safe."

"I can do that for a period of time, Mr. Holmes, but the boy cannot languish here forever. Sooner or later, I must either charge him or release him, and right now, I'd have to charge him. People will become suspicious and start to talk if I don't."

"Move him about if you must, but keep him safe. Now before I leave, I must ask your indulgence on another matter."

"In for a penny, in for a pound, I always say," Jones replied. "What is it that you need?"

"I should like very much to speak with the lad. I want to assure him that everything will be just fine and that his family will be taken care of. Will you do me that favour and bring him here?"

"Here? Why don't I just take you down to his cell?"

"Because people must think I have given up on the boy. If I am seen visiting him by the wrong person that could be disastrous."

"I understand," said Jones, who then left to fetch Wiggins. As soon as he had departed the room, Holmes darted behind Jones' desk, reached into the crate and extracted a silver watch on an ornate chain and put it in his pocket.

"Holmes, that is evidence," I exclaimed.

"You are most certainly right, and you may rest assured I will make much better use of it than the police ever will."

A minute or two later, Jones returned with Wiggins. Upon seeing my friend, the lad exclaimed, "I knew you wouldn't let me down, Mr. 'Olmes!"

"Gentlemen, if you will excuse us for a few minutes please?" asked Holmes.

"I'm not supposed to let the prisoner out of my sight," Jones said. "Suppose the doctor and I stand on one side of the room and you and Wiggins on the other?" And so it was that the inspector and I found ourselves huddled in one corner while Holmes conferred with Wiggins in hushed tones in another. "I wonder what that's all about," Jones inquired of me.

"Truthfully, Inspector, I have no idea. Holmes' request was as much a surprise to me as it was to you."

Several minutes later, the conversation ended and Holmes and Wiggins said their goodbyes. "Remember what I said, Wiggins. Keep your wits about you at all times. If you should require anything, ask to speak to either Inspector Jones or Lestrade – and only those two."

"Mr. 'Olmes. I'll be on my best behavior. I promise."

With that Holmes turned to Jones and said, "I am counting on you to keep the boy safe, Inspector."

"You have my word, Mr. Holmes."

We left Scotland Yard and hailed a cab. Although I was beside myself with curiosity, I could see that Holmes was in no mood for talking. He spent the entire cab ride with his chin sunk in his chest. In fact, he was so deep in thought that I had to rouse him after the cab had stopped at Baker Street.

As we entered the front hall, Mrs. Hudson came out of her kitchen. "Oh, Mr. Holmes, a letter arrived shortly after you left. The messenger said it was most important. You will find it on the dining room table."

Holmes practically bolted up the stairs, and I was not far behind. He strode to the table and carefully picked up the envelope which rested there. "It's the same paper as the previous message but a decidedly different hand."

As he slit the envelope open and removed the single sheet of paper, my curiosity got the better of me. "What does it say, Holmes?"

He simply handed me the letter. A single line of script bore the ominous message:

A pawn removed, Mr. Holmes! Advantage mine!

Chapter 12

"The cheek, Watson! The unbridled cheek!" he exclaimed. "However, I think I still have a few moves to make. In fact, I am certain that we are nowhere near the endgame. The question though is whom exactly am I moving against?"

Since I could render no answer to his last question, I just reaffirmed my faith in his judgment. "Just tell me what's to be done, Holmes."

"Good old, Watson," he said as he pulled the watch he had taken from Inspector Jones' office from his pocket. Opening the lid of the silver hunter, Holmes took his lens in hand and said, "You may recall that all pawnbrokers mark watches entrusted to their care."

I smiled ruefully recalling the occasion when Holmes had deduced a great many things about my unfortunate brother, based on the watch our father had left him. "I do," I replied.

"Some are more discreet than others and Jeffrey McKeever may be the most cautious of all. Knowing that some goods will inevitably change hands, McKeever, originally an artist by trade – and a rather talented one at that – marks them in a manner that is most inconspicuous. In fact, if you didn't know of McKeever's system, you'd have no idea the item had been marked, let alone where to look for the telltale signs."

With that he handed me his lens and the watch and said, "See if you can find his mark." I took the glass and examined every inch of the watch. I knew I was looking for markings of some type, but all I could discern were three tiny letters – TMA, presumably those of the jeweler who had fashioned the watch or perhaps its previous owner – inscribed on the inside of the lid at the very bottom. After about five minutes, I said, "I give up. Where are these hidden markings?"

"You must have seen them, Watson. You were staring right at them."

"The only thing I saw that appeared out of order were the initials TMA, and I presume they are the initials of the person who once owned the timepiece or barring that, the jeweler who made the watch. However, since they are rather unobtrusive, I'm inclined towards the latter."

"Once again, let me emphasise: There is nothing so deceptive as an obvious fact. The letters TMA are not the initials of the owner nor the jeweler, but rather letters from the Cyrillic alphabet. In that alphabet, letters also have numeric meanings taken from the ancient Greek. In this case TMA – Tau, Mu, Alpha – can be translated as 346 with T equaling 300, M 40 and Alpha 6."

"And this helps us how?"

"All we need do is examine McKeever's ledger and see who pawned item 346, and we will have the identity of our antagonist. McKeever has a shop on Fleet Street a few doors down from the far more reputable Suttons & Robertsons." Grabbing his coat, Holmes turned and said, "I am planning to pay Mr. McKeever a visit, if you should care to accompany me."

Needing no further invitation, I joined Holmes and some twenty minutes later, we alighted from a cab in front of McKeever's Merchandise Emporium.

When we entered, Holmes began to inspect the various cases. After several minutes of browsing, we were accosted by a clerk who asked, "May I help you gentlemen with anything?"

"Is Mr. McKeever here today?" asked Holmes

"He's in the back. Whom shall I say is calling?"

"Tell him an old friend has come to collect on a debt."

With that the clerk vanished, and Holmes and I turned to continue our examination of the watches and other items on display in one of the cases. A few minutes later, a sturdy, bearded man in his mid-forties, appeared behind us. "I don't believe that I owe you anything, sir," he said.

Turning around, Holmes replied, "That is quite true at the moment. However, you will be in my debt for what it is I am not going to do."

"Mr. Holmes," he exclaimed somewhat flustered at my friend's appearance, "to what do I owe the honour? And what is it you are not about to do."

"I should very much like to see claim ticket 346."

"You know I can't do that, Mr. Holmes, not even for you. A client is entitled to his privacy, after all."

"Watson, would you be so kind as to fetch the nearest constable? I shall wait here until you return."

"Now hold on, Mr. Holmes. Why are you sending for a copper. I run a legitimate business."

"That may be so," replied Holmes urbanely, "but I am fairly certain that at least two brooches and one watch among the items in your display cases have been stolen. You have been deceived, my friend, by one or more unscrupulous individuals. I am merely trying to see that the items are returned to their rightful owners."

There was a long pause and then as I turned and started towards the door, McKeever said, "What was the ticket number? 346?"

Holmes nodded and McKeever left us to return a few minutes later. "A silver hunter watch? Pawned originally in February of last year by a Mr. Robert Usher. He defaulted on the loan, and the watch was purchased in July of this year by a Mr. Ted Baldwin of Birlstone Manor."

I tried to conceal my emotions and watched as Holmes said, "Thank you, Mr. McKeever. You have been most helpful. In the future, I should try to be more circumspect about items on which you advance money. After all, there are those nefarious people who will try to take advantage of your good nature."

"I certainly will, Mr. Holmes, and let me thank you again."

"One more suggestion. Stick to the painting: I believe you have a rare degree of talent."

Once we were outside the store and a good distance away from it, I said to Holmes, "Ted Baldwin is dead. John Douglas admitted killing him."

"Indeed," replied Holmes, "yet I find the use of that name suggestive. After all, he might have chosen any name from the past such as Grimesby Roylott, Jack Stapleton, even Jonathan Small. Yet he chose Ted Baldwin – and it may be that bit of arrogance that provides the first lead to our foe's undoing.

"Of all the ne'er-do-wells we have encountered, Baldwin was the first one I could ever link to Professor Moriarty with absolute certainty – thanks of course to friend Porlock. It only remains for me to ask of him one more small favour."

"Do you think he will help you?"

"If the price is right, Porlock will do almost anything. Of course it will be up to me to minimise the risk and eliminate any possible chance of exposure."

"And just how do you intend to do that?"

"I am not certain yet, old friend, but the germ of an idea is beginning to take root. It only remains for me to let it grow and mature and flourish into a fully developed plan."

"Given the present fate of Wiggins and the attempt to have me imprisoned, might I suggest that you act with as much alacrity as is possible."

"You are correct, Watson. My greatest fear is that our foe will step up the attacks. My only hope is that with Wiggins under lock and key, he takes time to savor what he perceives as a small victory. If that is indeed the case, we may have earned a few days respite, but I am not optimistic."

As we would later learn, Holmes' fears were well-founded. However, he had picked up a scent, albeit a very faint one, and the expression on his face boded ill for any who crossed his path.

"So how will you contact Porlock?" I asked as we looked about for a cab.

"Our usual method is to correspond via the post. However, we did agree that in dire circumstances, I could attempt to reach him by placing an advertisement in the agony column of the *Standard.*"

"Surely you don't intend to address such a notice to the attention of Porlock."

Holmes stared at me incredulously. "Certainly not. To do so would be to sign his death warrant. There is precious little – and nothing of a criminal vein – that escapes the notice of Moriarty. It is amazing in that when it comes to matters of mischief and the criminal class, he seems almost omniscient."

I looked at him expectantly. Finally, he said, "You understand that this information can never be made public while Moriarty lives. Although it might make for one of your more entertaining literary endeavours, the fact is that people's lives hang in the balance. I am sorry, my friend."

I nodded my assent and said, "I totally understand."

At that he continued, "The notice will be addressed to Laverna."

"Laverna? Why Laverna?"

"First, the advertisement calls for the attention of a woman which is disarming in and of itself, but it's also appropriate since in Roman mythology, Laverna was a goddess of thieves, cheats and the underworld."

"My word, Holmes. What will you say?"

"I will ask to meet – which I am certain he will refuse. When we finally do make contact, I will ask for any information about this bogus Ted Baldwin and the attacks against you and Wiggins. He will reply with his price, usually around £10 or £20. In this case, I expect he will charge somewhat more. I will gladly pay it, and then we shall have our first solid clue in bringing this blackguard that has hounded us to heel."

"Do you think this thread will eventually lead to Moriarty?"

"That would be rather too much to hope for. No, Moriarty will cut it long before it even hints at his involvement. You must understand there are always layers of insulation between the Professor and those who perpetrate crimes on his behalf. My fervent hope is that we can capture his lieutenant, and the attacks will cease. After all, even criminals do not work for free – and the Professor is no exception in that regard."

I looked him with what must have been surprise on my face.

"Fear not, Watson. We shall have a reckoning with the good Professor at some point – sooner rather than later, I hope. For now, however, my primary concern is the individual who has allied himself with him."

The next evening, Holmes was working at his chemistry table while I was perusing the agony column of the *Standard* when I spotted what had to be my friend's listing. It read:

Dearest Laverna,
I must see you before I set sail.
Shall we meet at Solomon's Rookery
at 10 p.m. Friday?
Fidelio

Unable to make head nor tale of it, I studied it for several minutes before I heard my friend say, "Does its meaning elude you, Watson? I do hope so."

"I know you placed it because of the 'Dearest Laverna,' but the rest of it is just gibberish as far as I can see. I've never heard of Solomon's Rookery? Where or what is it?"

"I think our friend Mr. Dickins might take umbrage with your lack of knowledge in this instance."

"I know that a rookery is a home for birds. I also know that term is often used to refer to the slums wherein dozens of people are crowded into a single house, making the landlords rich. But Solomon's Rookery? I have been in some of the worst sections of London, and I've never heard of such a place."

"Quite possibly because it doesn't exist," he said with a smile.

"If it doesn't exist, how will Porlock find it?"

"To begin with, he won't accept the invitation, but on the off chance he does, I couldn't put the real meeting place in the notice, so I coded it."

"Well, it's a code that escapes me."

"Watson, what is my chief complaint about the police force?"

100

"You have many," I replied, at which Holmes chuckled.

"I suppose I do, but what do I maintain is their greatest shortcoming?"

"Their lack of imagination."

"Exactly. You know what a rookery is, now you simply need to connect one to a certain Solomon." He looked at me inquisitively, "No?" After I shook my head, he continued, "Many of Dickens' characters were modeled on people in his life, and the character of Fagin in *Oliver Twist* was inspired by the life of one Isaack 'Ikey' Solomon – a well-known ne'er-do-well of his time. At any rate, Fagin's home was near Field Lane. Should Porlock agree to meet, he will be able to figure out where and perhaps suggest a more exact location in his reply."

I was rather skeptical both of Holmes' plan and Porlock's ability to decipher Holmes' totally obfuscated hints. However I was proven wrong when the following day, the Standard contained this notice in the agony column.

Dearest Fidelio,
Solomon's Rookery square at 10 p.m.
Friday by stone corner. Take all appropriate
precautions.
Laverna

Holmes was nearly ecstatic, if such a word can ever be used to describe the man, at the response.

"I suppose you know what he means by 'stone corner'?" I asked.

"I believe that would be where Brickfield Close runs into Field Lane. Imagination, Watson."

"Yes, that and a thorough knowledge of London's byways," I thought, but I held my tongue.

"Despite my fears that it would never come to pass, Porlock has agreed to meet. With any luck this could lead to bigger things. Perhaps our reckoning with Moriarty will come sooner than I had anticipated."

Chapter 13

I was summoned to a medical emergency the next afternoon. A man had fallen from a loft and suffered a broken leg as well as various and sundry other cuts and bruises. When I finally returned to Baker Street, it was just in time to dine with a rather thoughtful Holmes. My attempts at conversation were rebuffed, and after dinner Holmes disappeared into his bedroom.

Some forty minutes later a weathered tar appeared in his bedroom doorway. In short, his disguise was impeccable. He sported stained corduroy trousers, work boots that were badly down at the heel and a faded peacoat that had a patch on one elbow. He had blackened his teeth, and a wicked scar ran down his right cheek. He completed the outfit with a worn wool watch-cap.

"Holmes, that is astounding," I said. "I don't think your own mother would recognise you."

"Let's hope no one recognises me," he said. "I have no idea when I shall return, so don't wait up for me."

Of course, those words fell on deaf ears. For a brief moment I thought of following him, but decided he would be angry and if anyone spotted me – I am not nearly so adept an actor as Holmes – his carefully constructed plans would be in ruins.

The old adage about a watched pot holds true in its own way for clocks. I tried reading, writing and playing solitaire, but nothing could distract me from constantly checking the time and nothing could ease the dread I felt for my friend.

Finally, just after one, I thought I discerned a stealthy tread on the stairs. I hadn't heard the front door open, so the thought crossed my mind that it might be a burglar. I reached over and armed myself with the poker, but it was for naught as Holmes entered the room.

Unable to restrain myself, I asked, "How did your meeting with Porlock go?"

"I didn't meet with Porlock," my friend replied irritably. "He sent a young girl in his stead."

"How on Earth did you know she was the one?"

"She was wearing a Phrygian cap."

"I still don't understand."

"The Phrygian or liberty cap, sometimes known as a *bonne rouge,* became a symbol of the French Revolution. As I am sure you know, Mozart's *Fidelio* was inspired by a true story from that dreadful period. At any rate, when I spotted the cap, I called out to her, 'Laverna?'

"She then came to me and said, 'And you are?'

"'Fidelio,' I replied.

"She inquired, 'You have something for me?' I then passed a small pouch containing five £10 notes. I then told her what I wanted to know. In turn, she said the information would be delivered in the post tomorrow. As she started to leave, I considered following her, but it was as though she had read my mind because she turned back and said, 'If you try to follow me, you will never hear from Laverna again.'

"So now I must possess my soul in patience until the morning."

"You should try to get some rest, Holmes. This case may prove to be a taxing one."

"You get some sleep, old friend. I have a few things to which I must attend before I do anything else."

The next morning I awoke earlier than usual and when I came down around quarter past seven, I found Holmes sitting in his chair in his blue dressing gown. His eyes were closed, and I thought he might be sleeping, but he disabused me of that notion when he said, "You are up early; I hope you slept well."

"I did," I replied.

"Mrs. Hudson should be along presently with coffee. In the meantime, I can do nothing but sit here and wait."

I glanced at my watch and said, "It's coming up on half seven, the mail will be here shortly."

About five minutes later, Mrs. Hudson appeared with the coffee, and said "This just came for you in the post, Mr. Holmes."

He practically snatched the envelope from the dear lady's hand, thanked her for the coffee and then ushered her from the room with all due haste. He then ripped open the envelope and pulled a single piece of paper from it. "What the devil?" he exclaimed.

"What is it, Holmes."

"Another of Porlock's puzzles." He then handed me the paper on which were written three names: John, Joseph and Madeleine.

"What does it mean?" I asked.

He didn't answer as he was scrutinizing the envelope with his lens. The letter had been posted from Finchley. Aside from his name and address on the front, the only other writing on the envelope were the words "Return of Post."

"I am missing something or perhaps several somethings. Why write 'Return of Post' when clearly no response is required? Why underline the R once and the P twice? Why post the letter from Finchley? Why include three disparate Christian names? Porlock has taken great pains to protect himself, and he's assuming I will be able to ascertain his motives and thus decipher the various clues.

"This is indeed a three-pipe problem," he pronounced as he reached for the Persian slipper that held his tobacco. Knowing that the room would soon be filled with the noxious smell of his shag, not to mention clouds of blue smoke, I excused myself, deciding to write a letter to my wife from my room. For her protection and my own, Holmes had refused to divulge her address in Wales – only telling me that she was safe, and that he would forward all correspondence from me to her and vice versa.

It was perhaps an hour later that I descended the stairs, finding the room much as I had feared. Holmes sat in his chair; thankfully, he was no longer smoking. His clipping books surrounded him on the floor.

"No luck?"

"The only link I can ascertain between the three names is that they are names. The two male names are fairly common, while Madeleine is far more popular in France than here. I have tried all manner of substitution ciphers to no avail."

After a pause, I added "It's too bad Porlock didn't think to include last names."

Holmes paused then looked at me. Suddenly, he exclaimed. "I have been a blind beetle. Porlock provided all the clues; it is I who missed them. The letter was posted from Finchley. Do you know what postal district that is? N3," he pronounced. Taken together, that would be London, N3 or LN3 or 'Last Name 3' if you will."

"I understand what you are saying but how does that help us?'

"It's quite simple: Can you not think of a common surname shared by a famous John, Joseph and Madeleine?"

I sat there thinking for a while and finally I admitted, "Nothing is coming to me Holmes. The first two as you said are far too common, and while the third should help, it still escapes me. However, obviously you have tumbled to something."

"Indeed, two of the three will be well-known when I tell them to you, but the third is the one that falls squarely within my milieu. I am a fool for not seeing it sooner."

He then smiled and said, "Might I suggest the surname Smith? As in Capt. John, of Colonial Virginia fame; Mormon founder, Joseph, with whom we have some small degree of familiarity; and socialite and accused murderess, Madeleine?"

"I have certainly heard of the first two, but the last one, not at all."

"In 1857 Madeleine Smith, a Scottish socialite, was accused of poisoning her lover with arsenic. It was a terribly messy affair. Ultimately she was acquitted but only because the prosecution had bungled the case terribly. Now, we take the once underlined R and the twice underlined P from 'Return to Post' and we end up with the name R.P. Smith."

"A relative of Culverton Smith?"

"It may well be although that will require some research before I can say so with absolute certainty."

With that, he threw off his dressing gown, grabbed his overcoat and hat and said, "I am off to the British Library. If you would like me to take care of that letter you've written to your wife, it would be my pleasure."

I thanked him and handed him the missive; it was only after he had departed that I wondered how he knew the letter was for my wife.

I stopped by my home and then spent part of the afternoon checking in on Dr. Fenton, the new locum who was covering for me. He had seemed a capable young man when we first met, and I soon realised everything seemed under control. After seeing a few of my regular patients and promising to visit and lend a hand when I could, I returned to Baker Street with a clear conscience.

About five, I heard the front door open and recognised Holmes' footfalls as he ascended the stairs. Trying not to appear overly eager, I let him settle himself in his chair, but before I could broach the subject, he said, "It appears young Dr. Fenton is getting along, and things are going smoothly at your practice."

"How could you possibly know where I have been?"

Pointing to the door, he said, "Old habits die hard. Your medical bag has returned to its place of prominence by the door. It wasn't there when I left this morning since you hadn't brought it from your home. I assume you can follow the rest of that chain of reasoning."

I nodded and said, "And as long as we're …"

"The missive to your wife?" he asked. I could only nod. He continued, "When you descended the stairs from your room this morning, I saw that the envelope was from your best stationary. Although the addressee was obscured by your hand, it was apparent that the letter bore no stamp. Since there are stamps on both your desk and mine, I can only assume you thought it would be delivered by hand – and in that respect, you are correct. It is on its way to her as we speak." He paused, "That should encompass everything, or am I missing something?"

"Your afternoon?"

He smiled, "Oh yes. Well it has been rather productive. Although I cannot prove anything yet, I am convinced that we are being hounded by none other than one Roderick Percival Smith.

"As you supposed, and I am inclined to agree, he is no doubt a relative of Culverton Smith. You will, I am certain, recall the name."

I thought back to the case I had titled "The Dying Detective." In it, Holmes had feigned being poisoned in order to trap Culverton Smith. Holmes had suspected Smith of poisoning his nephew, Victor Savage, in order to collect the inheritance. Determined to silence Holmes, Smith had sent my friend a small ivory box with a spring that had been laced with a deadly bacteria.

"Indeed, I do."

"But he's serving a life sentence in Pentonville Prison."

"He was – he passed away earlier this year."

"And who is this Roderick Smith?"

"A brother and a proper ne'er-do-well in his own right. He headed up a gang of thieves and pickpockets and was arrested in August of 1867. Unfortunately for him, after a speedy trial he was sentenced to ten years hard labor, and in September of that year, he set sail aboard the Hougoumont, the last ship to transport convicts from England to Australia. The Hougoumont docked in Fremantle, Western Australia, on January 9, 1868."

"My word, Holmes, "what an extraordinary tale."

"Sadly, Watson, it is only the beginning."

"What do you mean?"

"I need information, Watson. All I have now are suspicions. I cannot properly theorise without more data."

He paused and then continued, "Let us begin by consulting the barrister who handled Victor Savage's estate. After all, once Culverton Smith was imprisoned, he was no longer the heir, so let us see *cui bono*."

Holmes then summoned the buttons and despatched the lad to Lestrade with a letter, but on the way the youngster was to send several telegrams which Holmes had composed.

"It is rather late in the day, and I am not expecting any answers until Monday morning. Shall we dine at Rules and give

Mrs. Hudson the night off if she hasn't already begun preparing dinner?"

Chapter 14

Monday morning brought the two wires for which Holmes had been waiting as well as a letter from Lestrade, which was delivered by one of the local constables.

"Ah, at last," he said, reading the wire, "Victor Savage's estate was handled by one Charles Callari of the law firm Hastings & Walsh on Bishops Court, close to the courthouse."

"An appointment would seem to be in order," I suggested.

"I have no time for social niceties," he exclaimed. "Will you accompany me?"

Of course I agreed, and we were soon in a cab headed for the Old Bailey. When we entered the offices of Hastings & Walsh, Holmes asked for Mr. Callari. The receptionist inquired as to whether we had an appointment. Holmes said we did not and was politely informed, "Mr. Callari never sees anyone without an appointment."

"If you would be so kind as to give him my card, perhaps he will make an exception in my case."

The smug young clerk took the card and when he looked at it, he asked, "Is this a joke?"

"I assure you it is a matter of some seriousness," Holmes replied. The clerk scurried away and returned a few minutes later saying, "Gentlemen, please follow me."

We were led into a handsomely appointed office where a very prosperous looking man of perhaps fifty greeted us. He was about my height with a thatch of blond hair and a neatly trimmed goatee. "Mr. Holmes, what a pleasure it is to meet you." Turning to me, he said, "And you must be Dr. Watson.

"Gentlemen, please sit. Coffee or tea?"

Holmes declined for both of us, which then prompted Callari to ask, "How may I be of assistance?"

"I believe the late Victor Savage was a client of yours."

"Yes, and a good friend as well," replied Callari. "His death was a tragedy."

"Did you handle Savage's estate?"

"We did," said Callari. "Since his uncle was in prison for Victor's murder, the estate remained unsettled for several months. As you know, Victor had no immediate family here in England, but eventually we learned that Culverton Smith, his uncle, had a brother."

"Would that be Roderick Smith, late of Her Majesty's penal colony in Australia?" inquired Holmes.

"You don't beat around the bush, do you, Mr. Holmes?" asked Callari. "Yes, Roderick had been sentenced to ten years for petty theft and possession of stolen property. Although he maintained his innocence, he was found guilty and transported.

"Apparently, he remained there for a number of years after serving his sentence. During that time, I am told, he threw in with a bunch of Fenians who had been on the ship with him, and they all did quite well during the gold rush, both in New South Wales as well as Victoria.

"Among Smith's acquaintances were the bushrangers Harry Power and a very young Ned Kelly. As you can see, he has led a rather lawless life."

"Apparently, old habits die hard," I said.

Holmes shot me a reproving glance but Callari either hadn't heard or decided to ignore my remark. "Since you settled Savage's estate, have you heard any more from Smith?" asked Holmes.

"He has stopped by here on two separate occasions. On the first visit, he inquired about renting out Victor's home. I informed him that we did not handle that type of work."

There was a long pause and then Holmes said gently, "And on his second visit?"

"He asked me if I were interested in investing in a business enterprise with him. I explained that at the moment it would be fiscally imprudent for me to undertake such a venture."

"Did he explain what the business was?" inquired Holmes.

"Only in the vaguest terms."

"Did you recommend him to any of your friends as potential investors?"

"No," replied the attorney. "Truth be told, Mr. Holmes, there is something unsavoury about Mr. Smith. He is a rather loutish fellow, and he can be loud and uncouth at times. I was hoping he would be put off by my refusal, and so far it seems to have worked as I haven't heard from him in several months."

"Do you know where I can locate Smith?"

"As far as I know he uses both Victor's country estate and has his own rooms here in town. Let me check," the attorney then pulled open a file drawer and after shuffling through several papers said, "Here it is: Number 23 St. Ann's Terrace in St. John's Wood. I believe he was also renting out his brother's house in Lower Burke Street. Shall I write the addresses down?"

"No thank you, I think I can recall that," replied Holmes. "One last question, Mr. Callari. Did Smith give you any hint at all as to what type of business he might be opening?"

"I was under the impression that it was an import-export business," he replied. "I do wish I could be of more help."

"You have proven to be an invaluable source of information," replied Holmes.

"And this conversation stays between the three of us?" he inquired.

"Of course," replied Holmes. "Why do you ask?"

"I do not scare easily, Mr. Holmes. I served in the army and saw action in the Bombardment of Kagoshima. However, there is a ruthlessness about Smith, a subtle menace, if you will, that would give even the hardiest soul pause."

"I assure you that I will keep your words in mind should I have occasion to confront Smith – something I believe is inevitable."

After we had left the solicitor's office, Holmes said, "So what did you make of Mr. Callari?"

"He seemed a solid fellow, and I think you would do well to keep his words in mind."

Holmes said nothing during the cab ride back to Baker Street. When the driver let us off, I noticed a handsome Clarence across the street as I alighted. "I think you may have another case, Holmes."

Looking at the carriage, he said, "I think not but we shall see." With that he hurried up the steps and upon entering the house, he called for Mrs. Hudson. She came bustling out of the kitchen and Holmes said, "Has anyone called for me today, Mrs. Hudson."

"No, sir. The bell hasn't rung, and I would have heard it for I've been in the kitchen all morning baking."

"Thank you, Mrs. Hudson," he said as he bounded up the stairs. I could see that he was on edge, so I followed close behind. I don't know who was more surprised when Holmes opened the door – he or I – but I will confess to being taken aback at the sight of an elegantly dressed man sitting in Holmes' chair by the fireplace. He was smoking a cigarette, and a stranger might well have thought the rooms were his instead of ours, so at home did he look.

"At last, Mr. Holmes," the stranger said as he rose. "You have kept me waiting for some period of time. Dr. Watson, so good to see you again."

Taking the lead, I said, "Holmes, I'd like to introduce you to Dennis Mannery, I met him on my first weekend at Brucastle Abbey."

"Pleasure to meet you," said Mannery. "I'm afraid I took the liberty of letting myself in. Truth be told, I picked the lock on your front door. I'd strongly suggest you replace it with something a bit more secure."

Ignoring the man's comments, Holmes said, "Obviously, you two are acquainted. Might I suggest, Watson, you advise your friend that there are certain chances one takes when one calls unannounced and breaks into someone's home." Turning back to our visitor, Holmes inquired, "Mr. Mannery, may I ask what has occasioned this visit?"

"Mr. Holmes, my sincerest apologies," said Mannery. "I assure you no offense was intended, but I am being watched. You must have seen…"

"The Clarence across the street?" interrupted Holmes. "One could hardly miss it."

"The men in that carriage, along with several others on foot, have been following me for the past two days," he offered by way of explanation.

"So you decided to lead them directly here?" added my friend rather brusquely.

"Others were already stationed here," he replied evenly. "Your rooms have been under surveillance for some time now."

"I am well aware of that," replied Holmes. "New faces in Baker Street are not all that common, and there have been a veritable plethora of them in the past few months."

"Have you any idea who is watching you?" I asked.

"I can only assume they are members of some criminal organization," replied Holmes rather offhandedly. "I have made many enemies throughout my career."

"You are correct, Mr. Holmes. From what I have been able to gather, one Roderick Smith has taken a rather keen interest in you since you first took notice of Baron Leighton's activities."

"But you were a friend of the Baron's," I interjected.

"Friend might be stretching the truth a bit," Mannery replied. "I was investigating the Baron for the Royal Irish Constabulary. Our 'friendship' was merely part of my investigation. We had reason to believe that the Baron played a role in at least three murders in Ireland."

"I noticed you used the past tense, 'had.' Is that because the Baron is dead or because you have a new suspect."

"Your reputation doesn't do you justice," replied Mannery. "We know the Baron helped carry out the murders, even if he didn't pull the trigger, so to speak. However, since I began my investigation I have come to believe that he was working at the behest of another."

"And would this other person have a name?"

"Sadly, I have not been able to glean that nugget of information from any of my sources."

"I believe I may be able to assist you in that endeavor," said Holmes.

Chapter 15

"Have you ever heard of Professor James Moriarty?" Holmes asked.

When Mannery shook his head, Holmes continued, "I thought not. He was a professor of mathematics at one of our lesser universities, but he now works as an Army coach here in London." Holmes then gave a brief history of the man he believed responsible for most of the crime in London.

I was so caught up in his story that it took me several seconds before I realised he had stopped speaking.

"That's all well and good," replied Mannery, "and I am sorry for your troubles, but this Professor Moriarty is unknown to me and not wanted for anything in Ireland."

"I am confused," I said. "Since you have no interest in Moriarty and Baron Leighton is dead, why are you still here?"

"I am now looking for the person who killed Baron Leighton. As I said, the Baron was working for someone higher up, but I also believe he was working in concert with someone else in at least two of the deaths."

"Now, I am certain I can help you," said Holmes. "A moment ago, you mentioned Roderick Smith; what do you know about him?"

"Smith was transported to Australia. On the way there he became friendly with a number of Irish convicts, Fenians, on board the ship. That bond was cemented during their sentence and has continued even though they have served their time.

"Smith has let it be known that he did well in the gold fields. My informants tell me he ran a sizable criminal organization in New South Wales and would still be there had things not got a little too warm for him in that part of the country.

117

"He returned to England and then moved to Ireland for several years. Somewhere along the way he and Baron Leighton joined forces. At any rate, he was a regular at the Baron's soirees, which is where I first encountered him." Mannery paused here and then he said to Holmes, "Smith is a formidable foe, Mr. Holmes. Do not underestimate this man, for he is as cold as ice."

"So I've been given to understand, Mr. Mannery. In fact, you are the second person today to convey his concerns about Smith to me."

"If you should wish to contact me, Mr. Holmes, I have taken a room in Curzon Street. If your landlady has no objections, I will leave by the rear door that should give the watchers in the Clarence some pause."

"By all means. Watson, please escort Mr. Mannery out. I'll leave it to you to explain his presence to Mrs. Hudson, should she ask."

Fortunately, Mrs. Hudson was not in the kitchen when I spirited Mannery through it and out the tradesmen's entrance. As I made my way back upstairs, I must confess to being totally bewildered by Holmes' attitude. Here was a potential ally, yet Holmes had remained relatively non-committal.

As I was about to open the door, the buttons came out of the sitting room, carrying an envelope Holmes had entrusted to his care. I entered to find Holmes charging his pipe. Before I could say anything, he asked, "So what did you make of Mr. Mannery – if that is his real name?"

"He seems a solid enough chap. He was quite helpful on my first visit to Brucastle Abbey."

"If I recall correctly, I believe he told you that he and 'Freddy' – I believe that was how he referred to the Baron – were 'old friends.'"

"He did, but as he just admitted 'friends' might be stretching it a bit. I marvel at your memory, Holmes."

Ignoring my compliment, he continued, "And yet he was conspicuously absent on your next visit, was he not?"

"That is true."

"Most singular."

"He also said Smith was a regular at the soirees, but I didn't see him on either occasion."

"I'm certain that was by design and just because you didn't see him doesn't mean he wasn't there."

"Holmes, there are any number of reasons that might explain Mannery's absence – illness, a family emergency, a prior engagement – the possibilities are endless."

"I agree but speculation is pointless. I shall say no more until I know more."

With that pronouncement, Holmes proceeded to light his pipe and then curl up in his chair. When dinner arrived, he ate sparingly. It was shortly after eight that there was a knock on the door and Holmes yelled, "Come in, Mrs. Hudson."

"I was on my way up to clear the dinner plates when this arrived via messenger for you, Mr. Holmes."

"Thank you, Mrs. Hudson," he said with a smile as he handed her the laden tray in exchange for the wire. Opening it, he perused it several times, and then said, "There goes another promising avenue of inquiry."

He threw the paper on the table where I could easily read the response.

MAN IN LONDON AT BEHEST
OF RIC. STOP. PHOTO TO
FOLLOW VIA POST. STOP. A
GOOD MAN. STOP. POTTER

"I was rather hoping that Mr. Mannery would be something other than what he seemed, but it appears I was wrong. My old friend Inspector Potter has followed my directions and begun his reply with the first syllable of our new friend's alias. Also, he is sending a photo of the man for absolute verification."

"Well then, perhaps we have a new ally – both in this feud with Smith as well as your ongoing crusade against Moriarty."

"Perhaps, Watson. I fear it is far too early in the game to make any such assessment – but perhaps."

"Have you a plan?" I asked.

"I have been developing several – none of which seems to me satisfactory at this point. Thus far, we have not suffered directly at the hands of Moriarty, so my thoughts are much the same. I hope to begin by removing Smith from the board. Such a move will not only end this wretched persecution, but it will weaken Moriarty by depriving him of the services of one of his trusted lieutenants and a source of income."

"And how is that to be accomplished?"

"As the Bard might have noted, 'Ay, there's the rub!'" Following that exchange, Holmes threw himself into his chair once again, steepled his long, thin fingers under his chin and never moved except to refill his pipe occasionally. Familiar as I was with my friend's moods, I let him sit there in silence. I knew that he would share his thoughts with me only when he was ready, so after reading for a bit, I decided to turn in early.

When I rose the next morning earlier than usual, I learned that Holmes had risen an hour before me, had a single cup of coffee and dashed out the front door. With no pressing business, I stopped at my home and checked the post, visited my tobacconist and haberdasher, lunched alone at Goldini's, and checked in on my practice where I assisted Dr. Fenton for an hour or two. It was close on five when I finally arrived home and found Holmes sitting at his chemistry table.

When I entered, he looked at me with that all-encompassing gaze and said, "I see you have been as busy as I."

"I suppose you could recount my day for me, couldn't you?"

"Well I can see you stopped by your practice."

"How on Earth could you know that?"

"Your nose may have become oblivious to the scent of disinfectant, but I can assure you mine has not."

"Anything else?"

"You also visited your house to check the mail – the envelopes are protruding from your jacket pocket."

"Dash it all, Holmes. Is a man to have no privacy?"

"I'm sorry, old man. I shall go no further other than to ask how you enjoyed the fish at Goldini's?"

I examined my cuffs for stains, my boots and trousers for mud spatters, but I could see nothing that might have provided Holmes with a clue to my choice of dining spots, let alone my luncheon selection.

Finally in exasperation, I said, "I give up. How did you know?"

"I was sitting across the dining room from you; however, I rather doubt that you would have recognised me in my laborer's garb."

"You were there in disguise – working on the case?"

Holmes nodded. "You are right when you opined Mannery might prove an ally. My fear is that we are going to need several such individuals, and I was attempting to recruit another today."

"Are you going to tell me about it?"

"Not just yet, Watson. When I have all my ducks in a row, you shall be the first to know, I promise."

At that point, there was a tentative knock on the door, and Holmes said, "Come in."

The boy in buttons entered, holding a note, and said, "This just arrived for you Mr. Holmes. There's a constable waiting for a reply."

"A constable? What can this mean?" Opening it, he said, "It's from Lestrade; he would like to know if I will be home this evening as he has something he would like to show me."

Dashing off a quick reply, Holmes handed it to the boy. After we heard him clatter down the stairs, my friend said, "This must be a matter of some seriousness. Lestrade, as you well know, usually doesn't stand on ceremony. He frequently drops by without advance warning."

"All we can do is wait," I said.

We dined on roasted chicken with fresh greens and roasted potatoes. At exactly seven, the bell rang.

Glancing at his watch, Holmes remarked, "If he is nothing else, Lestrade is punctual."

A moment later, the inspector entered, carrying a small Gladstone bag, which he placed on the table. "This arrived in the post just as you predicted it might, Mr. Holmes. It came to the Yard this afternoon. I locked it in my drawer and have been quite careful with it ever since. The only time I touched it was to place it in the bag, and then I touched only the string."

Reaching inside the bag, Holmes removed a small package, wrapped in brown paper and secured with twine. Holding it up by the twine, he said, "Yes, it is as I expected."

Carefully cutting away the twine and the paper, Holmes then removed a small black and white ivory box with a sliding lid.

I had seen such a thing once before. "Why, Holmes, that looks like –"

He cut me off, saying, "Yes, it is a duplicate of the box I received from Culverton Smith. Had you opened this, Lestrade, I am afraid your life might have been forfeit."

"What do you mean?" exclaimed Lestrade.

"The box Smith sent me had a sharp spring inside that had been coated with a deadly plague. It would have cut anyone who unknowingly opened it and thus condemned that person to a slow, agonizing death. I was expecting such a ploy, and I see the apple doesn't fall far from the tree. Odd, I had given the man credit for more imagination than this."

With that, Holmes went into his room and reappeared with a long stiletto. After wrapping his hand and lower arm in towels, he eased up the lid with the knife blade while standing as far away as possible.

To our surprise and relief, nothing happened. Holmes looked at me with a quizzical expression on his face, but all I could do was shrug.

Looking into the box, he said, "There's a note and a chess piece." As Lestrade went to grab them, Holmes stopped him and said, "Just a minute, Inspector. One can never be too careful with something such as this."

Using a tweezer, Holmes first lifted the white pawn and then the note, which had been folded in two and then again, and placed them on the table in front of the box. He took his lens and examined the pawn carefully. It was a typical Staunton pawn from a smaller set, perhaps one inch tall. It appeared to be made of rather costly wood, but there was nothing distinctive about it that I could discern. Holmes then unfolded the note, still using his tweezers. Written on the paper were two words:

"What the devil does that mean?" Lestrade asked.

"It's a chess term," Holmes replied. "If you moved a pawn two squares forward on its first move because moving it only one would place it in jeopardy, your opponent has the option on his next move of capturing it *en passant* – in passing – as though you had moved it forward only one square."

"That's all well and good for those of you that play chess, but what does it mean and why send it to me?"

"I must admit its meaning escapes me at the moment, Inspector, but you see that someone is keeping an eye on you, so remain vigilant. Do not let your defenses lapse for a second, do you understand?"

"I am always on the lookout, Mr. Holmes. Should I tell the other inspectors about this?"

"Yes. Remind them that they should bring me any such suspicious package just as you did. The next one might not be as benign."

"Will do, Mr. Holmes," said the inspector as he prepared to leave.

"By the way, Inspector, have you had any luck in locating that Roderick Smith fellow, I mentioned to you?"

"Not yet, Mr. Holmes, but I've spread the word, and he can't hide from the law forever."

After he had left and we heard the front door close, Holmes turned to me and said, "This grows more serious by the day."

"So you know what message the chess piece and note conveyed?"

"Of course, don't tell me you haven't been able to discern its meaning."

"Well, unless I miss my guess, Smith is telling you that he could have removed Lestrade from the board as he did Wiggins, but he chose not to."

"Watson, that is it exactly. Bravo!"

I was taken aback at Holmes effusiveness as he tended to be rather parsimonious with his praise.

At any rate, I continued, "Thank you, but it's the why that eludes me."

"I think Smith enjoys toying with me, Watson. He knew Lestrade would bring me the package just as he knew that I had warned Lestrade. As you said, he wanted me to know that he could have removed Lestrade had he felt the urge. This is obviously some sort of gambit on his part."

"Then why not do it? Why allow you to keep an ally who may prove to be an asset later?"

"I am glad the inspector has left. I believe that Smith regards Lestrade as a pawn, a virtually valueless piece in many instances. As you know in chess, they are sacrificed routinely. As for allowing Lestrade to remain in play – removing him might have had far more serious consequences. After all, at the moment, it's a 'game,' if you will, between Smith and me. Removing Lestrade might have tilted the balance of power significantly – especially if all of Scotland Yard were to join the hunt as well."

"That is certainly an interesting way to look at it, but I repeat my earlier question: What's to be done?"

"You've played chess, Watson. What would you do?"

"This isn't a chess game, Holmes. It's real life with people – our friends –involved and at risk."

"I understand that, my friend, but I cannot say the same for our opponent. To him, this is nothing more than some sort of grand game, so I will play by his misguided sense of rules. In other words, I am going to castle."

"Do not wait up for me, old man. I may be out quite late." With that, he grabbed his hat, threw on his coat and was out the door.

Chapter 16

The next morning, Holmes was sitting at the breakfast table when I came down. "I was beginning to think you would never awake." Pouring me a cup of coffee, he said, "I trust you slept well. I fear that things are about to get a great deal more interesting – and uncomfortable – if you are still inclined to follow this case to its conclusion."

At that point, I noticed a small Gladstone bag by the door. Pointing to it, I said, "Are you going on a trip."

"Not so much a trip as a prolonged absence. I feel it may be in my best interest – and possibly yours – to quit Baker Street for a time."

"What? Where will we go? What will we do?"

"As you are well aware, I keep several hidey-holes throughout the city. I think it would be best if I made one of those our base of operations until we have captured Smith – and with any luck Moriarty as well."

"How will you manage it?"

"In a short while two men will arrive at the door. They will dwell here during our absence. Such an arrangement has the advantage not only of keeping our adversary off guard, but they can provide protection for Mrs. Hudson as well."

As you might imagine, I sat there dumbfounded. Then it hit me, "Is this what you meant by castling?"

"Exactly, the king moves to his left or right – the kingside or the queenside – and the rook moves one space past the king to protect him from an attack from that side."

I heard the bell ring and shortly after there was a knock on the door. Holmes yelled, "Come in, gentlemen," and two sturdy-looking fellows entered. Holmes introduced them as Messers.

Lange and Porter. Both were heavily bewhiskered and were bundled up in top hats, coats and scarves and carrying Gladstone bags.

"I shall be leaving shortly, Watson. If you wish to join me, you just have time to pack a bag."

Fortunately, as a veteran campaigner, I was able to put my kit together quickly and when I descended to the sitting room, I saw that two new men had taken the place of Lange and Porter and joined Holmes at the table. I was quite surprised and asked, "What happened to Lange and Porter?" Stepping forward, I extended my hand and said, "Gentlemen, I am Doctor Watson. It is a pleasure to meet you."

Holmes chuckled and said, "You've already been introduced, old man."

Looking closer, I realised that the two clean-shaven men standing before me had both sported full beards with side-whiskers not ten minutes earlier. "My word, Holmes. I congratulate you on your disguises, gentlemen."

They both laughed, and one – Lange, I think – looked at Holmes and said, "We had an excellent teacher."

"Now, if you would just sit here, Watson," said Holmes, indicating a chair at the dining room table, "We will make a new man of you."

With that, Holmes began to apply a sticky substance to my face and before long, I was endowed with a full, dark beard and moustache."

Disappearing into his room, Holmes returned a few minutes later, also bewhiskered. Holmes had his own bag, and I transferred my clothing into one of the Gladstones the men had brought. We then donned the hats, coats and scarves in which Lange and Porter had arrived and descended the stairs. A hansom was waiting for us, and Holmes instructed the driver to take us to the Lyceum Theatre.

After a few minutes, my curiosity got the better of me and I asked, "Who were those two men?"

"Let's just say that I have certain friends in the government to whom I may turn in case of an emergency."

"Well, it's quite fortunate that their coats fit us," I remarked.

"Fortune had nothing to do with it," replied my friend. "Lange is just about my height and build, perhaps a bit heavier, while Porter is much the same size as you. I requested those men specifically for that reason. With the shades drawn and a bright lamp on the table, their silhouettes in the window will closely match our own. It will be days before Smith discovers that he has been duped – if, indeed, he ever does."

About seven or eight minutes later, we pulled up in front of the theatre, and I recalled that this was where Holmes, Mary and I had met a driver who had been dispatched by Thaddeus Sholto in *The Sign of Four*. Holmes and I then switched cabs and Holmes gave the new driver an address on Brick Lane in Spitalfields.

As we drove off, Holmes said, "God willing, she will be home quite soon, Watson. But she is much safer where she is."

"Need I ask?"

"When we changed cabs, you let your gaze linger on the third pillar and a wistful look played across your features."

"I am an open book to you, am I not Holmes?"

He smiled and said, "Yes, but I must say it is a volume of which I never tire reading and in which I sometimes encounter the most unexpected surprises."

I was touched by this sudden and rare show of warmth from my friend, and before I could comment, he continued, "These will be tight quarters for several days, and you must do everything possible to curtail your snoring, Watson. I shall wake you hourly if I must."

Seeing that things had quickly reverted to normal, I merely nodded and said, "What is the plan?"

"We know that Baker Street is being watched, but I am not quite certain by whom as the watchers keep changing. We will return daily – I as a constable and you as a costermonger."

Before I could object and tell Holmes how much I hated these dress-up games, he cut me off. "It is a matter of life and death. We must force a confrontation with Smith. I have had the Irregulars, sans Wiggins, trying to locate him as well as my network of underworld contacts. He is either incredibly well-hidden or people are too afraid to divulge his whereabouts. Even Porlock maintains an ignorance with regard to Smith's location."

Before he could continue, the cab stopped and we stepped out at the intersection of Brick and Down streets. A few minutes later, we were safely ensconced in a ground floor flat on Down Street. It was a small room with two cots and three chests of drawers as well as a closet brimming with clothing of all types. On one wall was a large mirror.

"I see the purpose of this room at once. Enter as Holmes and exit as someone else entirely."

"Precisely! There is an alley in the back that leads to Grantham Place. You must remember always to use the rear door.

"Now, in the morning, you can pick up your cart at Higgins, the greengrocer, on Allsop Place and then stroll up Marylebone and onto Baker Street. Lange will go out every day at around 10 a.m. Porter will not leave until thirty or forty minutes later. I will follow anyone who tails Lange and you must do the same for anyone you see following Porter. Their rambles will take them to our favourite haunts where they will purchase books, tobacco and other sundries. They will repeat the actions with slight variations in the afternoon at approximately three o'clock and half-past.

"Once we know who is following them, we can, in turn, follow them when they are relieved, for I am certain our movements are being monitored both day and night."

"They key is subtlety," I remarked.

"Exactly, if you suspect that you have been discovered, you must break off the surveillance at once. Return your cart and then come back here. It is imperative that you make certain you are not observed when you return."

"I understand, old man. See but don't be seen. Hopefully, I've observed you closely enough to put your principles into practice."

"I have every faith in you, Watson. Now, I must go out as I have several errands to run. You can remain here or disguise yourself and do whatever you like – even accompany me."

I declined Holmes' offer and decided to spend the day reading and writing. Uninterrupted, the time passed rather quickly. I ate a solitary lunch, and Holmes returned shortly before six with dinner for both of us.

We talked long into the evening, and finally Holmes said, "Let us get some sleep; I'm afraid it will be five o'clock before you know it."

Inwardly, I groaned, for I knew that the days of rashers, eggs, toast with marmalade and second cups of coffee were a thing of the past for the foreseeable future.

It was dark when Holmes awakened me the next morning, and I donned the ragged pants, coat and hat that constituted the costermonger's costume. I had shaved my mustache the night before so as I gazed in the mirror, I was stunned at how different I looked. With a bit of a makeup – expertly applied by Holmes – I was no longer Watson, but Eddie.

I watched as Holmes donned the blue tunic and helmet of a constable. I considered asking him where he had secured it, but thought better of it.

We parted ways after a cup of tea at a tea shop, and the next time I saw my friend he was strolling along Baker Street. To the untrained eye, he was a bored Bobby walking his beat, but I knew he was taking in everything – and everyone. For my part, I was hawking apples, pears, grapes and figs. At exactly ten o'clock Porter – wearing Holmes' favourite hat and coat with the collar pulled up – left and walked in the direction of Marylebone Road. I must admit from a distance, he could have passed for Holmes. Some thirty minutes later, Lange, wearing my favourite coat and bowler, left and headed towards Park Road. Again, I was taken aback by his resemblance to me at a glance.

I saw no one follow either man – both of whom returned to Baker Street about an hour later. The charade was repeated in the afternoon, and again, I did not see any watchers. To say the day seemed endless would be an understatement. When Holmes and I compared notes that evening, he had nothing to report.

The next day was more of the same. The morning passed without incident and neither Lange nor Porter was followed as far as I could see. About two in the afternoon, a girl, perhaps ten or twelve, approached my cart. At first I thought she was simply a street urchin. She looked at me and asked, "No more apples?"

"I'm afraid you're out of luck, my dear, but the pears are quite good."

"That apple I had yesterday was bang up to the elephant," she exclaimed. "If you 'ave apples tomorrow, will you save me one?"

At that moment, it hit me. Holmes and I had been looking for men – and possibly women – but Smith had ripped a page from Holmes' book and was using youngsters to keep tabs on the occupants of Baker Street.

Fortunately, we had arranged a signal if we needed to summon one another, so as I walked down Baker Street, hawking my wares, I stopped and tied my shoe in front of 221B. By the time I reached Park Road, Holmes was waiting for me. I said, "Holmes, we have been seeking the wrong quarry. Smith is using street urchins, including girls, much like your Irregulars, to tail Porter and Lange during the day and possibly at night too."

"Excellent, Watson. You have outdone yourself. I was so busy looking for familiar faces from the demimonde that although I considered children briefly, I soon dismissed the notion."

At a few minutes after three, Lange came out of the door, and I watched as he strolled toward Marylebone with the young girl tagging behind unobtrusively. Forty minutes later, Porter appeared, and as he started in my direction, a lad of about fifteen fell in behind him.

Once the street was clear, I turned in my cart and changed my coat and hat. I was planning to follow the girl when she eventually left her post after Lange had returned, and I was hoping not to be recognised. However, I needn't have worried, for around six o'clock, a man approached the girl and spoke with her. He then made his way down the street where he stopped and spoke with two other youngsters. I was ready to take up the chase when an old priest bumped into me.

I said, "Excuse me, Father" to which he replied. "I have this. See if you can follow the children when they are relieved." With that Holmes set off in pursuit of the man while I spent another hour window-shopping and keeping an eye on the young watchers. I was beginning to wonder how much longer they were going to remain at their stations when a trio of youngsters – two girls and a boy – showed up to take their places.

As I walked by, I heard the girl who had sought the apple complain, "Same as yesterday. They both went out in the morning and then again in the afternoon. This is boring."

"You didn't say boring when you got your shillin', did ya?" asked the boy.

"No," she replied. She then ran down the street, joined the other two watchers who had been relieved and they all set out in the direction of Regent's Park. I was doing my best to keep up, but I was tired from two days on my feet and between skipping and running, their young legs soon left me far behind.

I was disappointed in myself, and I hoped that Holmes had fared better than I. Uncertain of what to do, I stopped in a public house where I had a savory meat pie and a tankard of ale. It was now dark, so I made my way to Grantham Place and thence to the flat.

It was empty when I entered, and, truth be told, I was glad. I sat on my cot reading, but before long exhaustion overtook me, and I fell into a sound sleep. I have no idea what time it was, but I felt someone shaking me and a voice saying, "Watson. Watson. wake up."

I sat bolt upright and saw Holmes smiling at me. "I can only assume the youngsters gave you the slip."

"No," I protested. "I just couldn't keep up with them. How did you make out?"

"Better than you, fortunately," he replied. "Our young man led me a merry chase. He took great pains to make certain that he wasn't being followed, but eventually I trailed him to a pawnshop on Walworth Road in the Elephant and Castle section.

"I considered venturing into the shop, but then I thought a cleric would be hard-pressed to explain his presence at a moneylender's. I waited outside for about forty minutes, but he never came out, so I can only assume he left by means of the back door. "

"Did you see any other children? The fact that anyone would employ them for something such as this, especially girls, is insidious."

"Having employed the Irregulars to carry out similar surveillance on several occasions, I find I cannot agree, Watson. Still, those young ladies, if I may use the term, are probably members of the Forty Thieves – and thus shoplifters or worse in training."

"The Forty Thieves?"

"I realise you do not frequent this section of London very often, Watson, and you are the better for it. The Forty Thieves, sometimes called the Forty Elephants, is an all-female gang that specialises in shoplifting. However, trust me when I tell you that some of these young ladies could put their male counterparts to shame.

"Fortunately, I have helped one or two of the members out over the years, and I think it is about time they repaid the favour. If they are involved with Smith, I'll soon know."

All the while Holmes was speaking, he was discarding his clergyman's clothing and donning the garments he wore when disguising himself as a sailor. After watching him alter his appearance with cosmetics, I was astounded at the change. He had been nearly unrecognizable earlier and now he was totally foreign to me.

"After I leave, wait an hour, and then you can return to Baker Street. Go in disguise, and use the rear entrance lest the young watchers realise they have been deceived. Thank Lange and Porter and tell them I shall be in touch if their further services are required. Ask them to disguise themselves and leave the same way you entered.

"Now, I am off to see my old friend Morgana, the current Queen of the Thieves."

"Good luck," I said as he departed.

He turned to me at the door and said, "You know I don't believe in 'luck.' I do believe, however, in well-constructed plans, and if all else fails, perhaps a generous bribe."

Chapter 17

Following Holmes' instructions, I made my way back to Baker Street where I relieved Lange and Porter. I think both men were glad of my arrival. Although they complimented Mrs. Hudson on her cooking, they did say that doing nothing all day was tedious at best.

I could tell that both were filled with questions, especially about the gun pockmarks in the wall, but they were too professional to say anything. After donning their disguises, they bid me farewell and unobtrusively slipped out the back door.

I waited up for Holmes, but when the clock struck midnight and there was still no sign of him, I decided to turn in.

The next morning I arose at eight and came down to find Holmes talking with a youngster, perhaps twelve years old. I heard him say, "… and tell Wiggins, just a few more days and he can once again lead the Irregulars. Now, you're sure you understand everything I've told you?"

Pointing to his head, the lad replied, "No worries, guv. It's all right 'ere."

With that, Holmes gave the lad some coins and the boy scampered out the door and clattered down the stairs.

After I heard the door slam, I said, "That certainly sounds like progress."

"Indeed, Watson. I had another most informative talk with Morgana last night, and now I know at least two places Smith is known to frequent. Sadly, even she could not provide me with the location of his lair. However, I do have the Irregulars on the case, and Morgana has agreed to keep up the ruse that her gang members are watching our every move."

"So they report to her and she reports to Smith or another go-between and you will follow whomever she meets with?"

"I see that a night's rest has done you good. You have it exactly. She gives a nightly report to one of Smith's men at either The Grapes on Narrow Street or The Prospect at Whitby in Wapping. Both are quite near the docks, which I find rather suggestive."

"I don't believe I have ever been in either,"

"I should hope not," replied Holmes. "They are two of London's oldest public houses and both have, shall we say, rather colourful histories.

"I plan to visit them this afternoon, and attempt to get the lie of the land. Although I rather doubt that Smith is using either, one never knows what one may discover. Then I shall return tonight and see if I can follow Smith's man back to his master."

"Do you think Moriarty will be nearby?"

"I am certain he will not. The Professor is never near the scene of any crime, and he always has several upstanding witnesses to vouch for his presence at the concert, lecture or gallery. That is part of the man's brilliance, Watson. He is never at the scene, but I can guarantee you, it is he pulling the strings."

"He sounds like a most formidable opponent."

"Indeed, he is. However, if I can weaken his organization bit by bit, silently, almost imperceptibly, then when I am ready all I need do is dislodge one timber to bring his entire house down upon his head. For the moment, that timber's name is Smith. Eliminating him will deal the Professor a considerable blow, and the best part is, he will still be ignorant of the fact that I have tumbled to his presence and his machinations.

"Now, I think another cup of coffee is in order and a quick perusal of *The Times*."

With that, he snapped the paper up and disappeared behind it. I sat there trying to think of ways that I might assist Holmes with this endeavour. We had seen so much together, and on more than one occasion he had saved my life. The idea of letting Holmes undertake this mission alone did not sit well with me, and I decided to tell him so.

Before I could speak, he said, "If you really want to help, Watson, you will remain here in case you should be needed. As the blind poet once wrote, 'They also serve who only stand and wait.'"

"Should I even bother to ask?"

"Your emotions are writ large on your face, old friend. After reflecting for a moment, you began looking around the room. Your eyes glanced at the pockmarks in the wall, then they moved onto my jackknife which holds my correspondence; finally, they shifted to the desk drawer where you are wont to keep your pistol of late. Your mouth tightened into a grimace before your face registered total frustration. It was obvious you were searching for a way to render aid, but no easy solution presented itself."

"After all these years, you still manage to amaze me, Holmes."

"And you me as well, Doctor," he said without further explanation before he disappeared into his bedroom. He reappeared around noon looking much like the tar he had disguised himself as for the meeting with Porlock. There were a few subtle differences, but I am not certain I would have recognised him were I not familiar with the garments he was wearing.

"I hope to be home for supper tomorrow. We will just have to see where this thread leads us. It is our first break in the case and I cannot afford to have it snapped."

The next day, I busied myself taking care of a variety of tasks I had been neglecting. I spent the better part of the afternoon trying to occupy myself. I tried organizing my notes on a few cases I had been meaning to write up, but I found myself unable to focus. Sometime later, thinking the threat must have subsided, I decided to enjoy the unseasonably warm weather and take a constitutional through Regent's Park. I was so enjoying myself that I decided to visit the zoo.

I had read in *The Times* that morning that a new Bengal tiger had arrived, and I decided I wanted to see the magnificent beast up close. I was just approaching the entrance to the zoo when a youngster ran up and said, "Dr. Watson, Mr. 'Olmes sent me."

Although I didn't recognise the lad, I assumed he was a member of the Irregulars. "What seems to be the matter, young man?"

"Mr. 'Olmes told me I might find you here, and 'e said 'e wants you to come right away."

Given his earlier demonstration, I wasn't at all surprised that Holmes had anticipated my visit to the zoo. "Where are we headed, m'boy?"

"Mr. 'Olmes has a cab waiting on Prince Albert Road. The driver knows where to go."

I followed the lad and saw a brougham waiting at the corner of Ormonde Terrace and Prince Albert. The driver, an ancient man who looked as though he and his carriage had both seen better days, looked down at me and croaked, "Be ye Watson, the doctor?"

"I am," I replied.

"Then get in!"

It wasn't until I had climbed aboard and my eyes had adjusted to the darkness that I noticed the shades had been drawn over the windows and then I saw a rather large man sitting opposite me with a pistol pointed at my chest.

"Don't cause a ruckus now, Doctor. It's not you we want but your friend, Holmes."

"Are you Smith?"

At that the man began to laugh. "No, but you will be meeting him shortly. I can guarantee that."

Gathering myself, I attempted to put myself in Holmes shoes. As we drove along, I tried to listen for different noises and to take notice of the sounds that creeped into the carriage. At one point, I was certain we were crossing over a bridge but I would have been hard-pressed to say which one.

After some time, we stopped. "It will just be another minute, Doctor." The driver then opened the door, and I realised I was in a barn or stable of some sort. I was led across a yard and through the back door of a house, shoved into a room and the door was locked from the hall. "It won't be too much longer now, Doctor," said the man through the door.

After perhaps ten minutes, the door was opened and the man with the gun said, "Just walk down the hall and no funny business. I don't want to hurt you but I will."

As we neared the end of the hall, a door on the right opened, and a genial voice said, "Come in, Dr. Watson."

I entered the room and was quite startled. Although Holmes had told me he was dead, I found myself staring into the face of Culverton Smith – only there were differences. Roderick Smith had the same high, bald head as his brother. The sallow yellow face, with its coarse-grained and greasy skin was identical. He also had the corpulent double-chin of his brother and the eyes, although sullen and menacing were a piercing blue. The major difference was in the body; where Culverton Smith had been a small, frail man – I remember thinking he might have had rickets as a child – his brother, Roderick, was tall and powerfully built.

Gazing around I saw there were a number of small tables set up with chess sets on them, and looking down I was startled to find that the rug I was standing on had been woven to resemble a chess board.

Gesturing to the room, Smith said, "It is my only vice. I neither drink nor smoke. I refrain from drugs and abjure the company of women. However, I will play sometimes for hours on end, perhaps days. I really don't keep track of time."

"You must be quite an accomplished player," I said.

"I am redefining the game. I eschew the offensive attacks and silly gambits so many players prefer today. I choose to focus on defense and when my enemies have come to me as they must do – then I attack mercilessly. I give no quarter nor do I seek it."

I was beginning to think that the man needed an alienist when he continued. "Yet as stimulating as these matches can be, they pale by comparison to the games I play against my adversaries. Your Mr. Holmes, does he play?"

"Although I am certain he knows how, I don't believe I have ever seen him at a chess board."

"More's the pity, for he has proved a worthy opponent thus far. Moreover, now that I have captured a key piece of his, I am curious to see how he will respond."

"I should hardly consider myself a key piece," I replied.

"Sadly Doctor, your considerations are immaterial to me; I am only concerned with those of Mr. Holmes. Now, we will see what type of energy Mr. Holmes will exert in order to secure your release. Dinner will be sent in to you presently. In the meantime, there are periodicals for your reading pleasure. I would provide you with writing materials, but we both know how easily a pen or pencil can be turned into a weapon."

With that, he sat down at one of the chess tables, and I was escorted back down the hall and shown back into the room where I was left to my own devices. After gathering my thoughts, I asked myself: What would Holmes do?

I began to examine my surroundings more carefully. The walls appeared sound, and there were no windows. The only items in the room were a lamp, a chair, a small table, a cot and several magazines.

As I searched my pockets, I began to despair. I had a few coins, some notes, my pocket watch and the clothes on my back.

A few hours later the man who had captured me brought me supper. Before he opened the door, he said, "If you want food, stand against the opposite wall and don't try anything funny."

I did as I was bidden and when he opened the door and saw that I had followed his instructions, I was rewarded with a meat pie and a small jug of water, which he pushed into the room on a tray. After he had locked the door and departed, I thought, "Finally, I have a weapon of sorts." I decided I would wait a while and ask him to refill the jug, and if the opportunity presented itself, I would try to bash it over his head and thus effect my escape.

However, around eleven, before I could put my plan into action, the door was thrown open and a man was literally hurled across the room where he collapsed when he hit the wall.

My captor grinned and said, "He was asking after you, Doctor, so we thought he'd like to join you."

I knew at that point it was Holmes in disguise, and he had deceived those ruffians just as he had fooled me on so many occasions. I went to him, knelt down and whispered, "Holmes, are you hurt?"

"I'm sorry to disappoint you, Doctor, but I'm not Holmes."

Chapter 18

The voice sounded familiar and then with a shock it hit me, "Mannery?"

"Just give me a few minutes, and I will be at your service, Doctor."

"What are you doing here?"

"Holmes sent me," he replied as he rose to his feet. "I believe he would have come himself, but I suspect he is rather occupied at the moment."

"What is he up to?"

"I cannot say with any great degree of certainty, I'm afraid. But he felt your safety was paramount so he despatched me."

Knowing that reticence was among my friend's foremost qualities, I totally understood his reluctance to share any more information than was necessary. "Does he have a plan to free us?"

"I am the plan, Doctor."

"How did they capture you?"

"I was asking after you in The Prospect at Whitby, and my questions aroused the ire of a gang of ruffians. Two or three of them went down," he said flexing his right hand as he examined the bruised knuckles, "but there were just too many and they overpowered me. They blindfolded me, put me in a carriage, and the next thing I knew I was being pitched across the room."

I must admit that I was distressed to hear Mannery's response. After all, my captor had been quite careful with me, and while we might outnumber him, I was almost certain that he would be accompanied by someone on future visits.

"What do they want with us?" I asked.

"I can't be certain," replied Mannery. "If I had to hazard a guess, I would say we are bargaining chips of some sort." As he said this he was removing the heavy woolen watch cap he had been wearing, and he extracted a small life preserver from the folds. "That's for you," he said as he handed me the blackjack. Seeing the surprised look on my face, he added, "They never think to check the hat." Before I could ask what he was going to use for a weapon, he took off his right boot and removed a piece of the sole, revealing a concealed knife. After he had reattached the sole and laced the boot back up, he smiled and said, "And this is for me." Taking in my surprised look, he added, "They may check inside the shoes but they never examine the soles."

Unable to believe what I was seeing and scarcely able to restrain my curiosity, I asked, "What exactly do you have in mind?"

Mannery then told me his plan, and we argued the pros and cons and tried to refine it – much as I have done on many occasions with Holmes.

The next morning, a voice from the hall said, "Breakfast, gents. Up against the wall where I can see you both or you don't eat."

Mannery and I took our positions and the door was eased open. He stood there looking at us, covering us with his pistol, and said, "That's it. Just behave and don't give Teddy any trouble and everything will be fine."

He pushed the tray in and started to close the door; at that point, I said, "Teddy, how would you like to earn £5?"

"I wouldn't let you out of here for £500. It'd cost me my life."

"All I want are some cigarettes. If you do that, here's the money."

I saw the smile on his face, and I began to think our plan might just work.

Teddy took the note and said, "I'll see what I can do."

He didn't return until that evening. There was a knock on the door and the voice from the hall said, "Up against the wall, boys. I have the cigarettes and your dinner."

We had extinguished the lamp so the room was quite dark. When Teddy opened the door, I was bathed in the pool of light from the door. Next to me, in the shadows, we had constructed a rude scarecrow by hanging Mannery's coat over the chair, which we had secured to the wall with our braces. In the darkness, it created just enough of an illusion.

Teddy was cautious. "Why is the lamp out?"

"It needs oil," I replied.

He then threw the cigarettes across the room, slid the tray in and started to close the door. "I'll be back later."

Before he could finish, I asked, "Do you have any matches?"

"Do you have any more money?" he replied.

"How much do you want?"

"I think another fiver should do it."

I turned to the scarecrow and said, "Do you have any money, Mannery?"

As Teddy waited to hear the response, he took a longer look at my companion. Stepping cautiously into the room, he asked "What's going on …"

He never finished the sentence as Mannery, who had been hiding behind the door, coshed him with the blackjack. We pulled him into the room, trussed him with our braces, which we had cut into strips, gagged him and relieved him of his gun.

"Now all we have to do is get out of here, and we can tell Holmes where Smith is hiding out."

We could hear other voices in the distance. However, I followed Mannery as he crept down the hall in silence, and we soon found ourselves in the alley behind the house. We soon made our way from Lower Burke Street to Fox Road and then to Newham Way where we hailed a cab. As we drove through Spitalfields and headed toward Baker Street, I could feel myself relaxing. Some forty minutes later, Mannery and I entered Baker Street where we found Holmes sitting in front of the fire.

Holmes rose and said, "Watson, it is so good to see you." Turning to Mannery, he said, "I am in your debt. Things went as planned?"

"Pretty much as you said they would, Mr. Holmes."

"Excellent," replied my friend. "I'm certain that Smith has moved his headquarters by now, but we won't know where he has moved for some time."

"You had agents watching his house?" I asked incredulously.

"You were in no danger, I can assure you."

At that point Mannery said, "If you gentlemen will excuse me. I shall be in touch tomorrow, Mr. Holmes."

"Thank you again, Mr. Mannery," said Holmes. "Once again, I owe you a debt that can never be repaid."

"If we can capture Smith, I'll be more than happy to say that our accounts are squared." With that, he opened the door and descended the stairs.

"Holmes, did you know that I'd be kidnapped?"

"I rather suspected an attempt might be made," he replied.

"Yet you did not think to warn me?"

"Had I warned you, I have no doubt you would have acted quite differently. I needed for Smith and Teddy and their friends to believe that you feared for your life. You could not have manufactured such fear."

"Still, Holmes, I feel that I have been ill-used – and by you, my dearest friend." I could see that he was stung by my words. For just a second the mask slipped, and I saw behind the façade that he so labored to maintain. Realizing that my complaint had touched him in much the same way that his using me for bait had irked me, I was hard-pressed to decide who was feeling worse.

Then the moment passed. "I know it's not much consolation, but trust me when I say that you were never in peril."

"How can you say that when you don't even know where I was taken and held?"

"You were taken to the house that once belonged to Culverton Smith on Lower Burke Street. You were taken in through the rear – which is why you didn't recognise it initially. You met with Smith in the front parlour where he keeps his many chess sets, and you were held in a windowless room at the end of the hall on the ground floor."

"My word, Holmes. You have it exactly! How could you possibly know?"

At that point, Holmes had turned away from me and was looking out the window at Baker Street. All of a sudden, I heard a croaking voice inquire, "Be ye Watson, the doctor?"

"You were the driver?" I exclaimed incredulously.

He nodded and smiled, "I've been working off and on for Smith for several weeks now. By the way," he inquired, "did Teddy ever give you your cigarettes?"

I could only shake my head and exclaim, "Holmes, you rascal."

"What did you think of Smith's chess room? Quite frankly, I don't know what else to call it."

"He certainly seems obsessed with the game. I'm certain you noticed the rug?"

Holmes merely smiled and nodded. "I am hoping his obsession may provide a means to his undoing."

"Why don't we have Lestrade charge him with kidnapping?"

"You entered the cab willingly, Watson."

"Yes, but I was then held at gunpoint."

"What would you say if I told you there were no bullets in the gun?"

"But how?"

"I told you that you were in no danger," and then changing subjects, he continued, "I suppose we could have Lestrade charge him with unlawful imprisonment, but such actions usually end up as a civil matter. Still, that may be an avenue worth pursuing if all else fails. At any rate, it would be your word and Mannery's against Smith's and Teddy's and Lord knows who else.

"No, Watson, I want him dead to rights, standing in the dock, facing a capital charge. It remains for me to tighten the nets and haul in our prey, but we have work to do before we can even begin to consider such a possibility with any degree of seriousness. And if I am quite meticulous in my planning, we may find a professor among our haul as well."

Having made his pronouncement, Holmes then charged his pipe and settled into his chair. I knew that he was planning and revising and rejecting and re-revising, so I left him to his own devices.

I was just nodding off in my chair when Holmes suddenly began to laugh.

"Are you all right, old man?" I asked.

"I think I shall soon be quite right," replied Holmes. "I have been struck by a thought of how to approach Mr. Smith and by extension, perhaps, Professor Moriarty."

"Would you care to share that insight?"

"How did I trap Culverton Smith?"

"By pretending to be ill and summoning him to cure you."

"Exactly. I deceived Smith, and now I must employ a similar strategy against his brother."

"Don't you think Roderick will be looking for some sort of trick?"

"Of course he will. That is why this plan must be foolproof. We are going to have only one chance to capture Smith, so we must make certain that we take advantage of it.

"In a chess game, to use his favourite metaphor, when your opponent makes an error – even one of the smallest magnitude – you must be ready to pounce. If you do not take advantage of every opportunity to capture a pawn or force him to move a piece when you are able, you are setting yourself up for failure later on.

"If I am able to pull these threads together and if they hold, our Mr. Smith may soon find himself entangled to such a degree that escape is impossible."

"And have you devised such a plan?"

"I have the outline of one, but it will require the cooperation of a number of people and, of course, secrecy is paramount."

"Would you care to share your thoughts?"

"Not just yet, old friend, but I will give you this to consider: 'The greatest enemy will hide in the last place you would ever look.'"

"Machiavelli?"

"No, Julius Caesar."

I was impressed with the ease with which Holmes had quoted the ancient Roman.

"I hope you can pull everything together."

"Hope is an expensive commodity. It makes better sense to be prepared."

"Caesar, again?"

"No, Thucydides. Now, I must think." And with that he threw himself back into his chair, laced his fingers under his chin and lapsed into what might appear to the casual observer as a state of torpor. However, long experience had taught me that those periods of apparent lethargy were quite often the calm before the storm. Rather than interrupt him, I simply headed up to bed. Holmes had made progress, and after so long tracking his quarry, I knew the hunt was about to begin in earnest.

Chapter 19

I slept well and awoke quite late the next morning refreshed, invigorated and ready to help Holmes in his quest to end this campaign against us. I must say that when I entered the sitting room, I was taken aback to see him in earnest conversation with an Asian man. Upon seeing me, Holmes rose and said, "Watson, so good of you to join us. Please allow me to introduce Michael Liu."

"It is a pleasure to meet you, Dr. Watson. I must admit to being a fan of your writing."

"Thank you," was all I could muster, as I had no idea why this man was in our rooms nor what he and Holmes might be discussing.

As though he had read my thoughts, something I knew Holmes was quite capable of when he was in the mood, he said, "Mr. Liu is a scholar and one of the world's foremost chess players."

So now I had an idea of why the man was here. Holmes continued, "He was born in China but educated in America."

"Yes, I took my degree at the University of Pennsylvania and considered attending medical school there."

"It's an excellent medical school," I remarked, "the oldest in America, I believe."

"That is so," replied Liu, "however I found the vagaries of the financial market far more alluring than the mysteries of the body, so I majored in finance."

"Mr. Liu is also, as I mentioned, a renowned chess player, and when I learned he was in London for a series of exhibition matches, I arranged a meeting."

Uncertain of what information Holmes might be willing to share with a relative stranger, I remained silent.

"Mr. Liu was just telling me how he employs many of the principles outlined in *The Art of War* during his matches."

"*The Art of War*?" I inquired.

"It is an ancient text, believed to have been written around 500 B.C. by Sun Tzu," Liu informed me.

"Never heard of it," I muttered.

"That's not surprising, Doctor, as the book has yet to be translated into English. However, there is a French version available if you are so inclined."

"And what does this Sun Tzu say about war?"

"First, you must understand that Sun Tzu was a great general. It is believed that in his 40 years as a commander, he never lost a war, a campaign or even a battle.

"Still it is an odd book in that he focuses on alternatives to battle as well as alternatives to war itself. For example, one of his most famous dictums is 'The greatest victory is that which requires no battle.'"

"I don't see how you can win if you don't fight."

"Sun Tzu focuses on various stratagems, such as delaying, using spies, making and maintaining alliances, employing deceit and being willing to submit, at least temporarily, to more powerful foes."

Looking at his watch, Liu said, "I would love to continue this conversation, but I have a match in two hours with Wilhelm Steinitz and I must prepare."

With that he rose, bowed to us and said, "Gentlemen, it has been a pleasure. Mr. Holmes, I do hope that information proves useful."

Holmes walked him to the door, thanked him and then closed the door behind him.

After he had departed, I said to Holmes, "Why do I know that name Steinitz?"

"Quite possibly because he is the World Chess Champion, the first official one I believe."

"And Liu is playing him?"

"I shouldn't be at all surprised if he defeats Steinitz, but only time will tell."

"And this book, *The Art of War*?"

"A remarkable tome. I had heard of it, of course, but I have never had the opportunity to actually peruse it, and now I do," he said, holding up a small leather-bound volume with a cover that read *L'art de la Guerre* in gilt lettering. "It is believed Napoleon was familiar with this volume. Some historians maintain his tactics of employing a direct attack, which could be repulsed with difficulty, followed by a 'smaller,' but more lethal surprise attack which would administer the coup de grace to the enemy, were borrowed from his Chinese predecessor."

"That is simply astounding," I replied. "I had never thought how similar your tactics are to those employed by the military."

"We are engaged in a war, old friend. We are fighting for the oppressed against those who would victimise them, abuse them, rob them and yes – even kill them."

I had never heard Holmes speak so passionately about his profession. Then as had happened on those few other occasions when he had let down his guard, the old, imperturbable, inscrutable Holmes returned. He looked at me and said, "I will say no more, but I will not be bested by these men."

He then turned and entered his bedroom, closing the door behind him. Perhaps he was annoyed with himself for allowing his humanity to emerge. Perhaps he merely wanted to read his new acquisition without being interrupted. At any rate, I decided to indulge my friend, and let him enjoy the solitude he claimed so often to desire.

By now, the morning was nearly over and as my plans were inextricably tied to those of Holmes, I decided to write to my wife. She had been a far better correspondent during her absence than I. Truth be told, I think I had received six letters from her while sending just two.

I began by apologizing for my neglect and then told her that hopefully we would see each other before too much longer. I was feeling quite pleased with myself and enjoyed the lunch that Mrs. Hudson had prepared. I yelled to Holmes that the food had been served and received nothing more than a grunt through the door for my efforts. I was glad to know that things were back to normal.

I was enjoying a delicious sandwich of cold beef when Holmes threw open his door. "I have been dense, Watson, almost insufferably obtuse, but I have finally devised a plan which I think may bring all this to an end." After that brief announcement, he returned to his room and closed the door behind him. To say I was bewildered would be an understatement, as I had no idea what Holmes had in mind.

However, I was not at all surprised, for I had learned from our years together that his muse spoke to him at all hours of the day and night. Now, I knew Holmes would refine and revise and test his plan repeatedly, and only when he was ready would he take me into his confidence. It was not a situation I enjoyed, but as Holmes had remarked on more than one occasion, I had "the grand gift of silence." So I returned to my lunch and decided to wait for orders, which I knew would be forthcoming in the not-too-distant future.

I saw no more of Holmes that day. Despite my entreaties, he did not come out for dinner, and though I stayed up until eleven o'clock, he remained in his room.

When I came down the next morning, I was uncertain whether to disturb my friend or to allow him to continue his silent ruminations.

When Mrs. Hudson brought up breakfast some twenty minutes later, I said, "You needn't bring anything up for Holmes."

"I didn't," she replied. "Mr. Holmes was up early and in rather fine spirits, I might say. After he had his coffee, he was out the door before seven."

"Did he happen to mention where he was going?"

"Does Mr. Holmes *ever* confide in me, Doctor?" she asked with just a hint of sarcasm.

"No," I replied, "and lately he seems less inclined to confide in me as well."

"Well, I'm sure he has his reasons," she said.

After she had left, I sat down to my place and was relishing the prospect of bangers and poached eggs, which I knew Mrs. Hudson would have cooked perfectly. Pouring myself a cup of coffee, I savored the strong taste and as I was returning the cup to the saucer, I noticed a small piece of paper that had obviously been concealed beneath the cup.

Certain it was a cleverly hidden message from Holmes, I unfolded the paper. To my surprise, it contained a single word that had obviously been written by my flatmate, for I recognised the hand. Yet the more I gazed at it, the more baffled I was. The only word on the paper was "*Zugzwang.*"

I was certain that its meaning bore on the case, else why leave it? Given the presence of the "Zs," I assumed the word was German in origin, so I searched through Holmes' books looking for a German dictionary – to no avail.

With my knowledge of German being extremely limited, I had no idea what the word might mean.

Fortunately, at that moment I heard Holmes' familiar tread on the stairs and decided to own up to my own shortcoming and ask him what it meant.

"Ah, Watson," he said as he entered, "I see you found my note."

"I do hope it isn't important, Holmes, for I have no idea what the deuce it means."

The smile on his face told me that he was enjoying the situation, but then he said, "I do apologise, Watson. There is no reason for you to be familiar with that word. At the moment it is used almost exclusively among chess players, and then only infrequently."

"Chess again," I muttered.

"Indeed," Holmes replied. "The game obviously has been a recurring theme throughout this case, no doubt occasioned by Mr. Smith's passion for the pastime."

"And what does this 'zug-zang' mean?" I asked.

"It's pronounced zug-zwan – the last g is silent."

I could see my friend was relishing this didactic moment, but I had reached my limit. "Holmes," I said through gritted teeth.

"Very well, then Doctor. *Zugzwang* is quite literally translated as 'move compulsion.'"

"What the devil does that mean?"

"That's quite a literal translation, but it's really more of an idiom. As you know, you cannot pass in chess. You must move a piece when it is your turn. In the endgame, a player might utter *zugzwang* to his opponent, which is a polite way of informing him that any move the opponent makes will only weaken his position further."

"And how does this apply to us?"

"Obviously, Smith feels that he has obtained a decided advantage over me, although I cannot possibly imagine what that might be. However, when next we meet, at some point, I plan to look Mr. Roderick Smith in the eye and say simply, *zugzwang*. I cannot wait to see the look of consternation on his face.

"Now, I have a bit of research to do in order to prepare for our tête-à-tête with Mr. Smith."

"You are meeting him?" I asked incredulously.

"Well, nothing has been formally arranged, but I am certain that our paths will soon cross in the near future, and I must be prepared for any and all eventualities."

Holmes then pulled down two volumes from his shelves, and I could see that this conversation had been exhausted. I spent the morning running a few errands. and then stopped by my surgery. As I was returning to Baker Street, I remembered I was nearly out of tobacco, so I made my way to my tobacconist where I purchased some Virginia blend as well as cigars and cigarettes. By this point, I was feeling benevolent, so I added some shag for Holmes to my order. By the time I returned home it was nearly one o'clock.

When I entered our rooms, I was not surprised to see Holmes in almost exactly the same position in which I had left him. However, in the time that I had been absent, it appeared as though several additional volumes had made their way onto the floor.

The fresh air had given me an appetite, and I was looking forward to lunch when I noticed that the breakfast dishes had yet to be removed from the table.

"Holmes, has Mrs. Hudson been up this morning?"

"I saw her earlier, Watson," he said vaguely, "and I know you did as well since I placed my note under your cup in her presence."

"Has she been up since then?"

"I really couldn't say. I had to attend to a small matter of business in Pall Mall. Since my return, I've been rather immersed in my books. Why do you ask?"

"It's nearly lunch time, and she has yet to remove the breakfast dishes."

"That is most unlike her," Holmes agreed.

He rang the bell for her, and when she didn't answer, he went to the door and yelled down, "Mrs. Hudson?"

The house answered him with silence. "Perhaps she went out to the market or is gossiping with one of her friends."

"If the dishes had been cleared, I would agree with you. But you know as well as I that she is not one to neglect her tasks."

"True, true." With that Holmes picked up his hunting crop and headed down the stairs. I was following close behind.

When he reached the bottom of the steps, he turned towards Mrs. Hudson's kitchen stopped and said, "Hello, what's this?"

On the door to her kitchen was a small envelope affixed to the wood with a drawing pin. After pulling the pin from the wood, Holmes freed the envelope and took out a single sheet of paper. Unfolding it, he read it and then handed it to me. It contained but three words that pierced me to the quick:

Pawn takes queen.

Chapter 20

"I cannot believe this," said Holmes. "I did not hear a sound, and although I was quite preoccupied, I am certain I would have reacted to any disturbance."

By this time, he had entered the kitchen, and I followed close behind. I noticed the rear door was slightly ajar. "Mrs. Hudson would never leave the house without closing and locking all the doors."

"Not voluntarily, at any rate," said Holmes.

I had been prowling around the kitchen looking for anything that might have given us an indication to what might have happened when Holmes suddenly exclaimed, "Please remain where you are, Watson."

I stood stock still and turned to see him behind me, down on his hands and knees examining the entrance to the door. "You can just see specks of sand here on the floor as well as on the outside step. Such sand as this can only be found down by the docks. Watson, see if Mrs. Hudson has had fish delivered this morning."

I looked around the kitchen and inspected the icebox. "There is plenty of meat, Holmes, but no fish."

"I was afraid of that. I can see it, Watson, as clearly as if I'd been here: There was a knock at the door, and Mrs. Hudson answered, thinking it was a tradesman making a delivery. At that point, she was quickly overpowered. She may have been drugged – although I cannot discern the rather distinctive aroma of chloroform – or she may have had a gun thrust into her face. At any rate, she was taken by force, and one of the men – for there must have been at least two – then pinned the note to the door."

As he was speaking, Holmes had stepped into the alley that ran behind the houses. "They might have gone anywhere in any type of conveyance. These cobblestones will tell us nothing."

"What's to be done, Holmes?"

"For the moment, he has the advantage. They must have still been watching the house and known that both the maid and buttons were off today. When they saw you depart, and I followed shortly thereafter, they decided to seize their opportunity. Had either of us returned in an untimely manner, at worst they would have had the upper hand by virtue of both numbers and surprise, so they took advantage of the moment."

"If he should harm Mrs. Hudson ..."

"He didn't injure you when he had the opportunity. No, old friend. I know you believe that I think everything revolves around me, but in this case, unfortunately, it does. From the very beginning, this has been about Smith causing me pain, making me suffer, for having brought his brother to justice. Were he not helped by Moriarty, I believe this whole affair would have been concluded by now with Mr. Smith enjoying a stay of untold duration at Newgate."

"Newgate?"

"It'll be the noose for Smith. If he did not kill Baron Leighton himself, he certainly had a hand in it. Now, just as he isolated Mrs. Hudson, we must do the same to him, and I believe I know how to accomplish that feat – best of all, I have been inspired by a chess stratagem."

Holmes then outlined his plan to me in general terms, and inspired might well be the best word to describe it.

A short while later that afternoon, I left the house and walked to Marylebone Road, where I hailed a cab driven by a familiar face. A short while later I was sitting in Lestrade's office.

After telling him about Mrs. Hudson, which elicited a shout of outrage from the good inspector, I began outlining portions of Holmes' plan to him. When I had finished, Lestrade looked at me, and I must admit that it was difficult to discern any reaction on the inspector's face.

Finally, he began, "What you are asking me is quite unorthodox, Doctor. I could well lose my badge and pension for it, especially if complaints reach certain ears. Still, I've never known you nor Mr. Holmes to give me anything but solid advice. Tell Holmes that although I have my misgivings, he can count on me."

I thanked the inspector profusely and told him that either Holmes or I would be in touch shortly with more specifics. "I would invite you to dinner tonight, but without Mrs. Hudson, Holmes and I must fend for ourselves."

"Don't you worry about that, Doctor. When this is over, we'll all enjoy a fine meal as Holmes fills us in on all the obvious things we have missed."

I had to chuckle at Lestrade's suggestion, but I knew there was more than a grain of truth in it. My cab had waited for me, and some time later I found myself back in Baker Street. When I entered the sitting room, it was obvious Holmes had gone out. The house was strangely quiet as we had contacted the kitchen maid and the page and given them both a week off, telling them that Mrs. Hudson had gone to visit her sister who had suddenly taken ill, and Holmes and I would soon be leaving for France.

I tried to keep myself busy to occupy my mind, but as the hours passed I began to worry about Holmes. Uncertain of what to do and with hunger getting the best of me, I had just started to pen him a note saying I had gone to my club when I heard the front door close followed by the sound of him ascending the stairs.

The door to our flat opened and Holmes entered in as jaunty – if such a word can ever be used to describe Holmes – a mood as I could ever recall. "You have had good news?"

"Let us just say that finally things appear to be falling into place. Obviously, I could wish that things had occurred with more alacrity, but there are times when one must be satisfied with one's lot."

"Would you care to tell me what has transpired?"

Pulling a book from his pocket, he remarked, "I have been considering the words of Sun Tzu." Opening to a page, he said, "I must admit I was particularly taken with this quote: '*Chaque bataille est gagnée avant d'être livrée*' or 'Every battle is won before it is fought.'"

"What the devil does that mean?"

"I shall leave you to ponder its significance old friend. However," he added with a twinkle in his eye, "what he says applies to chess as well as war."

"As well it should," I answered. After all, chess is little more than war on a miniature scale – but no one gets hurt or killed. Holmes, let me remind you once again, you are playing with people's lives, and the consequences of the choices you make are far more serious than simply removing a piece from a board."

"I am all too aware of the stakes, old friend."

And then it hit me that Holmes might be trying to put on a brave front for my benefit. I wondered if in Roderick Smith, he had finally met his match. I knew he considered the inestimable Moriarty a formidable foe. Perhaps between the two of them they had proved more than my friend – brilliant as he was – could handle. I stood there for a minute, taking in the enormity of the revelation that had just overwhelmed me. I was at a loss for words.

As I turned to Holmes, searching desperately for something to say, I found him looking at me with a bemused expression on his face. "I do hope that after all we have been through together, you aren't going to start doubting my abilities at this stage of the game."

"The thought never crossed my mind," I lied.

Despite the situation, Holmes allowed himself a brief smile. "To continue employing the terminology of 'the royal game,' we have finally arrived at the endgame. Smith believes, having abducted Mrs. Hudson, that he now holds a significant advantage."

"He doesn't?"

"Not at all, Watson, There are forces at play here of which Smith is unaware, and I am confident those same forces will prove to be his undoing as well as that of Professor Moriarty."

At that point I began to wonder if Holmes had involved his brother and all that he might bring to bear in this affair. Thinking back to the sudden appearance of Porter and Lange, I was certain Mycroft had rendered aid and assistance. Now I found myself wondering about the extent of his involvement. I made a note to ask my friend at a more propitious time and returned to the subject at hand.

"If, as you say, the Professor is always miles away from the scene of any crime with an iron-clad alibi, I fail to see how these events could lead to his undoing – to use your word."

"I should hope you do not, old friend. Please try not to be offended, but if you could divine these plans, I am afraid they would not be worth much in a battle such as this."

I must admit that I was taken aback by my friend's directness. I knew Holmes had meant no disrespect, so I put my feelings aside and soldiered on, remembering that Mrs. Hudson's safety was of paramount importance – and that any slight hurt I might feel when confronted by a cruel truth paled by comparison.

"So will you not share your plan with me?"

"Not just yet, old friend. We are near the end – not at it," he replied. "Trust me, you shall know all when the time is ripe."

"And in the interim?"

"Might I suggest a late lunch at the Holborn?"

"An excellent suggestion. I am rather famished."

"We must make one stop before then," said my friend.

After we had entered the cab, Holmes told the driver to take us to Hatton Garden.

We took a cab and sometime later we alighted at the intersection of Greville Street and Hatton Garden. Holmes walked down the street and stopped in front of 102; the sign proclaimed the premises as the home of "T. and J. Jaques, Wholesale Ivory Turners."

The window was filled with various items, including several chess sets, but pride of place had been given to a number of croquet sets. "Really, Holmes? A toy store?"

"The sign hardly does them justice," explained my friend. "In addition to croquet sets and other such things, they work not only in ivory but in various exotic hardwoods, and they produce croquet mallets, false teeth and chess sets. In fact, John Jaques, while he didn't invent the game, was instrumental in popularising croquet when he displayed his complete sets at the Great Exhibition of 1851."

"My word, I never knew."

"However, I am here because they also produce a number of Staunton chess sets."

"Staunton, I am vaguely familiar with the name. Didn't he design the pieces that bear his name?"

"Actually, he did not. The pieces, with which we are all familiar, were the brainchild of Nathaniel Cooke. He was the editor of *The Illustrated London News,* for which Howard Staunton, who was the top player in the world at the time, wrote a chess column. Cooke asked Staunton to promote the set which he did, and in gratitude Cooke named it after him."

By this time, we had entered the store, and one of the clerks came forward and greeted us. "So good to see you again, Mr. Holmes. By the way, you missed a splendid match the other day. Michael Liu played Wilhelm Steinitz to a draw. Things were looking bad for Mr. Liu but then Steinitz was forced to sacrifice his queen and shortly after that, they agreed to a draw."

"I'm so sorry I missed it," replied my friend, "but I understand you have some good news for me."

"It arrived yesterday from Ireland. I'll fetch it for you." He returned in just a few minutes, carrying a chessboard and a mahogany box that obviously contained the pieces. "There you are, sir. You can see the signature right here," he said as he opened the box.

I looked on as Holmes pulled out his lens to examine the inside of the lid. There I could see, even without a lens, the name Howard Staunton writ bold. The ink had faded somewhat over the years, but there was no mistaking the signature. Next to it was the numbering, "1/500."

After he had finished examining it, Holmes exclaimed, "Perfect. I trust everything has been taken care of."

"Indeed it has, sir. If you should ever decide to part with it, I would appreciate it if you would give us right of first refusal. These sets are so rare – and this being the first of a limited lot – no one ever gives them up unless they are absolutely desperate."

"Or the price is right," I thought.

"You have my word," replied Holmes.

As we headed for the door, Holmes stopped, turning back to the clerk, he asked, "Are you familiar with Roderick Smith?"

"Indeed, I am, sir, and I must say if he ever finds out that you have the first signed Staunton, he's going to be beside himself."

"Well, I certainly would like him to see it. Perhaps you would be so kind as to deliver a note for me."

"I don't know where he lives," replied the lad, "but he comes in at least once a week or sends someone in his stead. If it is nothing too urgent, I will see that he gets it."

"Thank you," said Holmes. He produced an envelope from his jacket pocket, quickly wrote a note which he placed in the envelope which he then sealed. He then handed the envelope to the lad along with a sovereign. "For your trouble," he said.

"It's not necessary, but it is appreciated. I'll make certain that he gets it as soon as possible."

Although we might have walked to the Holborn, I insisted that we take a hansom. When we were safely ensconced in the cab, I asked Holmes, "What are you going to do with that?"

"With any luck, I'm going to checkmate Smith and end this harassment once and for all."

"And is that the bait?"

"You saw his 'chess room,' Watson. He is truly a fanatic, and I do not think he will be able to resist the lure of a signed Staunton set – especially since I now possess the only available one of its kind; moreover, it has the singular distinction of being the first set signed by its namesake."

"Holmes, I do not think that I should like to play chess with you."

"To paraphrase the Bard, and I'm afraid abuse his work rather soundly:

'*The set's the thing*
with which we'll catch this conscienceless king.'"

Chapter 21

After a leisurely meal, we returned to our rooms at Baker Street. As we stepped into the hall, I noticed an envelope on the floor. When I picked it up, I saw that it was addressed to Holmes. "Well that didn't take long," I remarked.

"I didn't think it would," he replied evenly. "We've been under surveillance all day."

Before I could say anything, I heard from the kitchen, "Oh Mr. Holmes, Dr. Watson! I'm in the kitchen. Please help me!'"

As we entered the kitchen, I saw our landlady bound to a chair

"Mrs. Hudson, what are you doing here?" I asked, as I set to work undoing the knots that held her wrists. While I was freeing her right wrist, Holmes was busy examining the knot that secured her left.

"Tied with a clove hitch but with a variation – one end has been passed under the other, forming an overhand knot under a riding turn, which suggests to me a mariner."

"For God's sake, Holmes, will you free the poor woman?!"

"My apologies, Mrs. Hudson. I was hoping the bindings might provide a clue to your abductors."

"No apologies necessary, Mr. Holmes. As for your question, Dr. Watson, I am not quite certain, sir. Two men came in with my lunch about two hours ago, and when they returned to take away the dishes, they told me I would be returning to Baker Street shortly."

"You were not mistreated?" I asked.

"Not at all, Doctor. It was rather like a holiday – except I was confined to my room."

"Do you know where you were held?" asked Holmes.

"I was blindfolded as soon as I was taken, and again on my return. However, I can tell you that the ride lasted between thirty-two and thirty-five minutes,"

"My word, I exclaimed. How can you be so precise?"

"I looked at my pendant watch right before I heard them entering the room to fetch me and then again, as soon they deposited me at the door."

"Splendid," remarked Holmes.

"Yes, during the drive, we crossed a bridge, though I'm afraid I cannot say for certainty which one."

"Would you recognise any of your captors?"

"I'm afraid not, Mr. Holmes. Every time I was in their company, they wore masks. I might recognise their voices, but I couldn't swear to it."

"They didn't hurt you in any way?" asked Holmes.

"The only thing that has been injured is my pride," she said forcefully. "They said they left a note for you in the hall, Mr. Holmes."

"Yes, I have it, dear lady," said he. "I think your ordeal is over."

"Hardly an ordeal," she replied tartly, "more of a minor inconvenience. Now if you gentlemen will leave my kitchen, let me take stock of it and see what I can prepare for dinner tonight."

Looking around, it suddenly hit her, "Where are Edna and Billy?"

"After you were taken, we thought it would be safer for them if they remained at home for a few days. I will send for them tonight, and I'm sure they'll be here bright and early," I told her.

"Bless you, Doctor," she said as she ushered us out of her domain.

When Holmes and I had got settled in, I said, "What did the note say?"

"It's from Smith. In exchange for freeing Mrs. Hudson, he has challenged me to a game of chess."

"You can't be serious," I exclaimed. "After everything he's done, he wants to play chess?"

"What exactly has he done? More to the point, what exactly can we *prove* he has done?"

"He tried to frame me for murder, for starters. And he killed Baron Leighton."

"Any witnesses, Doctor? Any proof?"

"Dash it all, Holmes. He had me kidnapped."

"Yes, and it will be your word against his and Teddy's and anyone else he feels like suborning. He'll say you were drunk and broke into his house, and they'll swear to it."

"What about Mannery?"

"Same thing. No, Watson, it won't do. He's played this game quite carefully so that anything he has done will be a case of your word against his and several other stalwart witnesses."

"What about Mrs. Hudson?"

"She doesn't know where she was taken, and her captors all wore masks. That's another dead end I'm afraid."

"So what's to be done?"

"I fear I must accept Smith's invitation and see where it leads us."

Holmes read the letter a second time and then mused, "It's actually rather flattering."

"Flattering," I exploded, "surely you jest."

"Not at all," my friend replied unperturbed. Smith says that many people regard me as a genius – or to use his words, 'some sort of savant.' He goes on to say that while he has tested

173

himself against all the greatest players in the world, he has come to regard me as the only 'great intellect' – again, his words not mine – with whom he has yet to do battle.

"I wonder if he and the Professor play chess," mused Holmes, more to himself than anyone else.

"You realise he's appealing to your well-known 'vanity' – my word, not his – and this is nothing more than a trap."

"No doubt you are right," Holmes replied, "still if I could find a way to turn this to my advantage."

"Where does Smith intend you contest this game?"

"He's invited me to his home and has offered to send a carriage. And if that arrangement is not to my liking, he suggested the recently formed Battersea Chess Club, which meets in the Bellringers' Room, on Vicarage Road, Old Battersea. He will secure the premises for the evening. He said I should be able to contact him by sending my response to Jaques of London."

"Will you accept then?"

"I will if I can turn the meeting to my advantage, but meeting at his choice of locale would be akin to ceding him the high ground – something I am loath to do.

"No, Watson, let me not make a precipitous decision but ponder the possibilities. After all, every offering is rife with possibilities just as in chess every move can lead to an untold number of countermoves – if only we can recognise their true potential."

With that he pulled out his cherrywood pipe which had served him well on so many occasions, filled it with shag and tamped the tobacco down. After lighting it with a taper, he then curled up in his chair and slowly the room began to fill with smoke. Knowing conversation would be impossible for the foreseeable future, I left him to his ruminations and escaped to my bedroom where I began composing another letter to my dear Mary. I started by telling her that I thought we were nearing the end of this ordeal – and our separation.

However, at some point I closed my eyes to relax for a few seconds and must have dozed off, for it was quite dark when I heard Mrs. Hudson announce, "Gentlemem, I've prepared a rather late dinner for you."

I descended to find Holmes sitting at the table. As I took my seat, our landlady lifted the top from a silver platter and proclaimed, "You won't find roast beef better than this anywhere in London – not even at Rules or any of those other fancy places you like to dine at occasionally." After that last remark she gazed pointedly at Holmes.

Initially I thought Holmes, who had been preoccupied all evening, had ignored her remark. Suddenly, he snapped out of his brown study, looked at her and said, "I am certain you are correct, Mrs. Hudson, and by the way, thank you very much."

"For what?" she inquired. "I've made you dinner many nights without so much as a nod and tonight a 'thank you.'" Beaming, she replied, "I'm sure you're welcome, Mr. Holmes. Now enjoy your meal." With that she curtseyed and departed.

"Pray tell, what *was* that all about?"

"Sometimes, my muse speaks to me from the most unlikliest of sources. Mrs. Hudson has inspired me. I know now how to turn Smith's invitation to my advantage. It only remains for me to finish weaving my net, and then we will have him, Watson. Now, if you would pass that delicious looking piece of beef, I shall carve."

To say I was dumbfounded by the sudden change in demeanour of my old friend would be to understate the matter gravely. In an effort to regain my mental equilibrium, I said,

"Obviously, I have missed something of import. Would you care to enlighten me?"

"You heard what I heard; you know what I know. Now is the time to give free rein to your imagination as you are so often wont to do – despite my misgivings – when chronicling our little adventures."

As we ate I wracked my brain, trying to figure out what Mrs. Hudson might have said or done to rouse Holmes from his lethargy. I could tell from the occasional slight smile that played across his face that Holmes was enjoying my discomfort. Finally, he took pity on me and said, "Mrs. Hudson mentioned Rules and I believe her words were 'other fancy places.' Now, Watson, think! We are seeking an advantage in our chess game ..."

"Simpson's," I exclaimed. "The Bishop's Room."

"Bravo," exclaimed Holmes.

"I understand that you have shifted the game to your preferred meeting place – assuming Smith accepts."

"Given the history of the place, I cannot picture him refusing, Watson"

"Yes, but I don't see how trading one chess club for another turns things in your favour."

Holmes then explained how he hoped things would proceed, and when he had finished, I could only shake my head in disbelief. "You are risking a great deal – your reputation, possibly your life – and if you should lose..." I let my words trail off.

"But I have no intention of losing," he assured me, "especially when the stakes are so high."

"And what will you be playing for?"

When Holmes told me, I could only shake my head in disbelief.

He looked at me, smiled and said, "What is it Kipling says:

'If you can dream—and not make dreams your master;
If you can think—and not make thoughts your aim'

"Trust me, old friend, my dreams, such as they are, will never be my master."

Chapter 22

The next morning, Holmes was waiting for me at the breakfast table. "Watson, we have much to do and little time in which to do it."

"But, Holmes, it's just past eight."

"I have been up since six. I sent the page to the telegraph office at seven. I have also written two letters, which the lad is delivering as we speak. Now I am confined here while I wait for replies, one of which should be coming shortly as I instructed the youngster to wait for an answer. Until I hear further, I can do no more."

Having made his pronouncement, he buried himself in the morning papers. I was enjoying my breakfast and had just finished a second cup of coffee when I came across an article in *The Times*. "My word, Holmes, did you see this story about Garrard & Co."

"No, I must have missed it," he replied. I thought his response odd given the way he devoured the daily newspapers searching for articles that might portend the beginning of a case, but I put it off to his having so much to do with Smith and his constant harassment.

"Pray tell, what happened, old man."

"There's not a great deal of detail here, but it says a manager at Garrard & Co. discovered that a small shipment of precious stones, which were to be made into a necklace for Her Majesty, has gone missing. All told, sixteen jewels of varying sizes cannot be found. They included eight diamonds of the first water, four rubies, two sapphires and two emeralds."

"I suppose we shall have to look into that as soon as we have put this present business behind us."

"Holmes, this is the jeweler to the Queen."

"I am well aware of Garrard's long association with the Crown, but I am trying to bring a dangerous criminal to justice. So I can either devote my time to tracking down some missing baubles, costly though they may be, or closing the books on a criminal who has confounded us for far too long. If you were in my shoes, Watson, which would you pursue? Besides, from what little you have told me I am almost certain that it was what Lestrade likes to call 'an inside job,'"

I hesitated for a few seconds and during that brief interlude I suppose my silence spoke volumes. Before I could answer, I heard the front door slam and then the sound of young feet bounding up the stairs. The door was thrown open and our page ran across the room and thrust an envelope into Holmes' hands.

"I got back here as fast as I could, Mr. Holmes."

"Thank you, my boy," replied Holmes, slipping a few coins into his palm.

Tearing open the envelope, he read it over and a short smile played across his face ever so briefly. "Things are falling into place. Now there are a few things to which I must attend personally. I may be out until supper. Shall we dine at seven here or would you rather the fare at Simpson's?"

"I should prefer to eat here in the comfort of these rooms where we can talk freely."

"Excellent, Watson." He then entered his bedroom and came back out a moment later carrying his small Gladstone bag. As he was putting on his coat and hat, he continued, "To your point, I believe we may have a great deal to discuss before tonight's entertainment. I shall see you at seven."

With that he was gone, before I even had the opportunity to ask him about the "entertainment."

With little to do, I spent the day helping out at my practice. I think the locum appreciated my assistance as it gave him some free time to take care of his own affairs.

After a day of tending to various coughs and sneezes, a sprained ankle, one case of gout, and two cases of lumbago, I returned to Baker Street eager to see what the evening held. Holmes was waiting for me when I arrived and said, "Tonight, I hope to bring to an end Smith's reign and perhaps do some damage to Moriarty's network."

"How do you plan to do that?"

"As I told you earlier, I am going to make the stakes irresistible so that Smith will have to accept my offer."

"And what exactly will you be wagering?"

"Among other things, I intend to place that Staunton chess set that Mycroft was kind enough to procure for me as my half of the wager. If Smith wins, he gets to keep the set, but if I win, all forms of harassment will cease."

"Holmes, Smith is by all accounts an incredibly accomplished player. By the same token, I have never seen you sit down to a board in all the years I have known you."

"Watson, as you have observed, chess is akin to engaging in war. There are no casualties as you also pointed out. There is no real risk – except perhaps to one's pride. Every case I have undertaken is like playing chess with lives and reputations hanging in the balance. How often have I told you that I had devised several plans for accomplishing my goal? The key is the ability to anticipate your opponent's move and, if possible, to be at least three or four steps ahead of him.

"I am certain that Smith is an excellent chess player; he may even have given the legendary Staunton a run for his money, but I am just as confident in my own ability to out-think and out-scheme Mr. Smith."

"I do hope you are right, but even if you should win and Smith does stop hounding us – there is still no justice. You believe him to be involved in the murder of Baron Leighton, and he may have played a role in the murder of John Russell, who died a horrible death in the Tower Bridge – and Lord knows how many other people he has killed or harmed."

In reply, Holmes smiled and said, "If I may quote our old friend Sun Tzu one more time: 'The wheels of justice turn slowly but exceedingly fine.'"

Holmes refused to elaborate on his cryptic pronunciation. Truly, the man can be maddening at times. After dinner, he said, "We'll be leaving at a quarter after the hour sharp, so please be ready," and then he disappeared into his room.

I looked at the clock and saw that I still thirty minutes to fill. I wondered whether my army pistol might be necessary and decided having it couldn't hurt. By the time I had cleaned and oiled the gun, it was ten past the hour. I descended the stairs just as Holmes emerged from his room, carrying the Gladstone bag again.

"Excellent," he pronounced, "punctual as ever."

We donned our coats and hats and descended the stairs to the street where a hansom was waiting for us. At two minutes to eight, we stopped in front of Simpson's. I took in the tiled exterior, done in black and white to resemble a chess board, and thought about the long association of Simpson's and the "royal game." The manager, Edmund Cathie, greeted us as we entered. "Mr. Holmes, Dr. Watson, so nice to see you again. You are expected, and everything has been arranged exactly as you ordered."

With that, he escorted us down a flight of stairs to what was commonly known as The Bishop's Room. Looking around, I noticed that the room had been arranged with a single table in the middle and a row of chairs perhaps ten feet behind where each player would sit and another row of chairs stretching across a third wall about five feet from the players. I took a seat here as it would afford me an unobstructed view of the board. Once I was seated I realised there was a second table with a pitcher of water and glasses for the players

Smith was sitting at the table waiting for us. "At last, you're here. So nice to see you again, Dr. Watson."

I could only stare and marvel at the utter brazenness of the man.

"I was beginning to think you had changed your mind," Smith said to Holmes.

"Not at all," replied Holmes. "A bit more traffic than I had anticipated."

"So, for the ground rules. We shall play three games, best two out of three – if a third match is required. Should a fourth or fifth match become necessary because of draws, we will continue until we have a winner."

"Agreed," replied Holmes.

"Shall we use clocks, Mr. Holmes? I have brought a set, and they are becoming an integral part of the game."

"If you wish," replied my friend.

"You know there is a ninety-minute limit?"

Holmes merely nodded his assent.

"Finally, shall we employ the touch rule?"

"Certainly," replied Holmes.

"And we know the stakes?" Holmes nodded.

"Have you brought the Staunton set?"

Holmes opened the Gladstone bag and extracted the chess board and box he had picked up from Jaques of London. Smith examined the box, and just as Holmes had so often done, he pulled a lens from his pocket while scrutinizing Staunton's signature and the numbering.

"These sets are extremely rare, and for you to have the first of the first limited run – astounding! I don't think I should have agreed to your terms under any other conditions. May I ask how you acquired it?"

"You might say it's been in the family," replied my friend.

"Always the coy one, Holmes."

"Shall we play with it?" asked Holmes.

"I would be delighted," replied Smith. "It will also give you an opportunity to say farewell to all your little friends individually."

With that Smith took a black pawn and a white pawn, turned his back to us and then turned around again, extending two closed fists as he did so. Holmes tapped Smith's left hand which he opened to reveal a black pawn. "I will play white. It would appear as though you have given me the advantage already, Mr. Holmes."

I will not bore you with the details of the games; however, the first two were closely contested matches. Smith won the first game with a knight move that put Holmes into check while pinning my friend's queen. At that point, Holmes resigned.

In the second game, Holmes played white and used what I later learned was the Staunton Gambit while Smith played what I later learned was the Sicilian defense. Again, it came down to the endgame, where Holmes was left with one pawn to Smith's three but its position on the rook file allowed it to advance and become a queen. Smith resigned two moves later.

The players agreed to a short break before the third game. While Smith was enjoying a whisky, Holmes asked for coffee. The final game was also a touch-and-go affair, but at the start of the endgame, Holmes, who had been smoking cigarettes incessantly throughout the evening, had a sudden coughing fit. He rose to get a glass of water and when he sat down he accidentally jostled the table with his leg, and knocked over his rook which he then reset on its base.

At that point, Smith pounced. "I am afraid you touched your rook, Mr. Holmes."

"Inadvertently, as a result of my clumsiness. I touched it only to place it upright."

"We did agree to touch chess, did we not, Dr. Watson?"

"Yes, but…"

"There are no exceptions. I am afraid I must ask you to move the rook."

The rook had been protecting Holmes' king and when he moved it, Smith immediately captured it with a pawn.

The odds had certainly tilted in Smith's favour, but before he made his next move, Holmes looked at Smith and said very softly, "*Zugzwang.*"

Smith began to laugh. "I do admire your sense of bravado, Holmes, but no amount of bluffing will save you. I see mate in three moves."

Smith was as good as his word, and three moves later Holmes was forced to concede. "You are a worthy adversary, Holmes, but I'm sure you can appreciate the fact that all's fair in love and war."

Holmes said nothing; he merely glared at Smith, who continued to prattle on, "Now, you are a man of your word, so you have one week to quit London. Good night, Mr. Holmes, and as I rather doubt we will be seeing one another again, let me also say good-bye." With that he left carrying the chess set which Holmes had brought with him.

When we were alone, I asked Holmes, "What did Smith mean when he said you had one week to quit London?"

"That was also part of the bet," Holmes said. "We agreed the loser would leave London and not return so long as the other one was living in it."

Chapter 23

You might have expected me to write that the cab ride to Baker Street was a dismal affair – spent in sullen silence. However, nothing could be further from the truth. While I was in a veritable state of turmoil internally, I could only admire my old friend's stoicism and his refusal to complain about his defeat. In fact, after we had arrived at our rooms, Holmes said, "I think a nightcap is in order."

He then poured us each a glass of whisky, and we sat there in silence for some time. I was trying to remember every detail of those moments, for at most I had but a few of these nights left with my friend.

"Holmes, where will you go? What will you do?"

He looked at me and smiled enigmatically, "I shall continue to do what I have always done. As for going anywhere, I am quite content with our rooms here in Baker Street."

"But Holmes, the wager with Smith. You promised to quit London if you lost."

"Actually, Watson, we agreed that the loser would leave London and not return so long as the victor is living in it…but suppose the victor is living somewhere else? I would think that would allow me to return to London – having only to depart should Smith return."

"I suppose there is a certain logic to what you say."

"And that is all I'm going to say for this evening. Now, good night, Watson. I have a busy day ahead of me tomorrow."

"Holmes, you are far too cheery. I know that you have something up your sleeve."

"I'll give you a hint, Watson, when I said *zugzwang* to Smith, I meant it. Had he heeded my warning, things might have turned out very differently." With that he bade me goodnight and entered his bedroom.

Left alone with my thoughts, I tried to put myself in Holmes' place. Quite obviously I had missed something – presumably something of significance – but wrack my brain as I might, the solution eluded me.

The next three days I saw little of Holmes. We took no meals together, and it was as though we were strangers who would pass each other occasionally exchanging only a pleasant word or two and little more. Always one to keep irregular hours, he carried that practice to new heights in the days following his ill-fated match with Smith.

I was beginning to worry as the week that he had been given to leave London was rapidly drawing to a close. Late that Thursday afternoon, I heard the bell ring, followed a moment later by a knock on the door. I opened it and was surprised to find Lestrade standing there.

I invited him in and he looked about and said with genuine surprise in his voice, "Mr. Holmes isn't here?"

"No, he's been in and out a great deal the past few days, and I haven't seen much of him. Did he ask you to meet him here?"

"Actually, no. I just thought he might be interested in the latest developments with the Smith case."

"Developments? What's going on, Lestrade? Has Holmes told you that he has to leave London?"

"You mean because of the bet? I believe he mentioned something about it. Doctor, please tell Mr. Holmes that we are picking Smith up tomorrow at noon, and that the other thing – he'll know what I'm talking about – has all been arranged.

"Also, tell him I'm sticking my neck out for him and he had better be right or it might well be my job."

More confused than ever, I promised Lestrade that I would relay his messages to Holmes. However, the inspector added one more puzzling remark just before he left: "I often wonder how Holmes knows the things he does. Do you think he might tell me how he tumbled to this one?"

Obviously Holmes had taken Lestrade into his confidence regarding some key aspect of the case. Not wishing to appear totally at sea, I told Lestrade, "I am certain Holmes will explain things when it suits him – he always does."

"That's certainly the truth. Well good night, Dr. Watson," Lestrade said as he closed the door behind him.

Unease and confusion were vying for control of my emotions as I sat in front of the fire, which had been allowed to burn itself to ashes. I poured myself a brandy, looked at my watch to discover it was half six, and reconciled myself to another meal in solitary silence.

I waited up until nearly midnight but Holmes never returned. When I came down for breakfast, he was sitting at the table, perusing the papers. "I trust you slept well," he said.

"I might have slept better if I knew what was going on. You have promised to leave London, and you haven't even begun to pack or make any arrangements of which I am aware.

"By the way, Lestrade stopped by last night." I then relayed the inspector's messages, adding my suspicion that Lestrade now knew more about the case than I did.

"I do owe you an apology. Trust me when I say I have been busy putting things in order. Speaking of which are you free this morning at eleven o'clock?"

"I was going to stop home, but if you need me, I will be there."

"It was not so much a question, old friend. It's just that I don't think you'll want to miss this."

Thoroughly mystified, I pressed Holmes for an answer, but he kept changing the subject. "They appear to have made significant progress on the Tower Bridge since this affair began," he offered.

"You're changing the subject," I replied, without looking at him.

Taking a different tack, he said, "According to *The Times*, they still haven't figured out who made off with the Queen's jewels."

"It won't work, Holmes. If you're not going to take me into your confidence, I will just have to possess my soul in patience until eleven o'clock."

The next couple of hours were spent in an awkward silence. Finally, at about a quarter to the hour, Holmes entered his bedroom; he emerged some ten minutes later and said, "I think it's time we set out."

When we reached the bottom of the stairs, Holmes asked me to wait a minute, and he walked and knocked on Mrs. Hudson's door. She opened it and said, "I'm ready, just as you requested Mr. Holmes."

To say I was nonplussed would be an understatement. When Holmes opened the front door, I saw a coach pulled by two glossy black stallions waiting for us at the curb.

"Punctual as ever, Jimmy," Holmes told the driver.

With that Holmes opened the door for Mrs. Hudson who climbed in. When I followed, I saw that there were two other people already in the coach. When my eyes had adjusted after a second on two, I recognised Wiggins and Mannery.

"So you're no longer in custody?" I asked the youngster.

"I've been out for nearly a week already, thanks to Mr. 'Olmes. But I've been keeping out of sight."

"And it's good to see you again, Mr. Mannery."

By this time, Holmes had taken his seat, and the coach had begun to move.

After he had made the necessary introductions, I addressed Holmes, saying, "I don't suppose there is any point in asking where we are going."

"I thought you rather enjoyed surprises, Watson. I'm fairly certain you'll like this one."

We passed the next hour in amiable chitchat, and Wiggins was particularly entertaining as he told us stories of the Irregulars and some of the plights they had found themselves in because of Holmes. Even Mrs. Hudson, who often looked askance at the leader of Holmes' street Arabs, seemed to be enjoying his tales. Finally, the carriage stopped and the driver said, "We're here Mr. Holmes."

Looking out the window, I realised that we were at the far end of Lower Burke Street where it ran together with Fox Road. Up the street, I could see a police wagon. I turned to Holmes and started to say, "Isn't that …"

"Just watch," he told us.

A minute or two later, Lestrade and Gregson exited the house. Between them was Roderick Smith in handcuffs. "I didn't do this," Smith was bellowing. "I'm innocent."

I heard Lestrade reply, "You may be a great many things, Mr. Smith, but innocent certainly isn't one of them. Now come along quietly. I don't want to have to get rough with you."

Holmes looked at Mannery and said, "I am sorry to disappoint you, but I can guarantee you that Smith will get his just deserts in an English court of law."

"I'm indebted to you, Mr. Holmes."

By this time the inspectors had bundled Smith in the wagon, which then started towards us on its way to Scotland Yard. As the wagon drew even, I could hear Smith still proclaiming his innocence.

He was standing in the back, hanging onto the bars and screaming, "I've done nothing." When he saw Holmes, who had stuck his head out one of the windows, Smith bellowed, "This isn't over Holmes – not by a long shot. You will rue this day." And then the wagon started up again, and all we could hear were his curses and protestations.

With a smile on his face, Holmes announced, "Justice has been served." Speaking more to Mrs. Hudson and Wiggins than Mannery and myself, he continued, "That man, Roderick Smith, whom the police just arrested, was responsible for trying to frame Dr. Watson for murder; for having you arrested for theft, Wiggins; and for abducting Mrs. Hudson. I am certain that he has committed a great many other offenses, including possibly murder," he said, nodding at Mannery, "but those are the ones that most concern me."

I was sorely tempted to ask Holmes on what charge Smith had been arrested, but as I looked at him, I discerned an almost imperceptible shaking of his head, and I knew that my query would have to wait.

We then shared a celebratory lunch at Simpson's, and Holmes was in rare form playing the genial host. Just as dessert was being served, we were joined by Inspector Lestrade. Holmes ordered the inspector coffee and advised him, "No talking shop,

Inspector. We are here to celebrate. Should you care to drop by this evening, I will be more than happy to answer any questions which you and the good doctor should care to put to me."

Lestrade could see there was no point in arguing with Holmes, so he acquiesced. However, as we were leaving, he gave it one final try, "Just one question, Mr. Holmes. How did you know where he had hidden the stones?"

"Lestrade, I promise that I will answer all your inquiries to your full satisfaction – inasmuch as I am able without compromising my sources – this evening."

"Then I'll see you at eight, Mr. Holmes. Again, you have my thanks and those of the folks at Garrard's – as well as Her Majesty's, I'm sure." He then bid the rest of us farewell.

I could see the policeman was unhappy, but I also knew that having been credited with apprehending the man who had stolen the Queen's jewels that he would wait until the evening for his answers – after all, he really didn't have much of a choice. But his questions echoed in my mind: How did Holmes know Smith had stolen the jewels – let alone where he had hidden them – and where had he concealed them?

After we had returned to Baker Street, Holmes had the coach take Mannery to his hotel and Wiggins to his family's stall in Portobello Road. Mrs. Hudson thanked Holmes again and promised us something special for dinner the next evening. "I don't think you'll be wanting a full supper after that lunch, so I'll prepare something light this evening – perhaps sandwiches – in case the inspector hasn't eaten. Tomorrow will be a different story, gentlemen." With that she went down the hall and into her rooms, but I noticed there was a confidence in her step that had been missing.

Holmes and I headed upstairs, and although I tried to get him to discuss the case, he said he preferred to go through it just once, with Lestrade present, rather than explain things now and have to repeat himself later.

Seeing that I was somewhat crestfallen, he said, "I'll give you another hint, Watson. You can make of it what you will."

"Fair enough," I agreed.

"It was a 'poisoned pawn' variation." Having made his pronouncement, he picked up the paper, settled into his chair, lit his pipe and lapsed into silence.

Chapter 24

Having only a passing familiarity with the game of chess and being totally unfamiliar with its finer points, I had no idea what a "poisoned pawn" might be, let alone a variation of the same. I decided to visit my club in hopes of finding Thurston there. From all accounts he was a fairly accomplished player, and on the one or two occasions when I had obliged him, he had bested me rather easily.

I found Thurston practicing in the billiard room, and after we had played a few games, I asked him if he had ever heard of a "poisoned pawn," but he shook his head. "That's a new one, Watson. However, I will admit that the term is suggestive on several levels. Presumably, any piece could be 'poisoned' if you wanted to use that term. I'm guessing it means you are sacrificing a piece for some tactical advantage later in the game, but I'm just guessing. Still, I don't see any other explanation."

"No, I'm certain you are on the right track."

"Perhaps you could visit one of the chess clubs this evening and see what the players there make of it. They have some first-rate players at the Battersea Club, and I'm sure you can find someone at Simpson's to help you."

I knew it would be too late to visit a club that evening since Lestrade was due at eight, and I was pretty certain that Thurston had put me on the right track. I sat there by the window, smoking, watching the passersby below and trying to figure out exactly how Holmes had entrapped Smith.

As was often the case, my ruminations yielded little. I knew something significant had occurred during the match, but I was hard-pressed to point out exactly what it was.

I returned home around seven and found Mrs. Hudson had been as good as her word. There was a tray of meats and cheeses and two loaves of freshly baked bread.

"And did anyone at your club know what a 'poisoned pawn' is?" asked Holmes.

"Do you never tire of these parlour tricks?"

"They are not tricks, Watson. I prefer to think of them as exercises in deduction. The philosopher Blaise Pascal once observed, 'Chess is the gymnasium of the mind.' My 'parlour tricks' are simply mental calisthenics in the art of deduction."

"And how is it that you deduced that I was at my club – as opposed to the library or my tobacconist?"

"The blue chalk dust on your left cuff is a rather telling give-away," chuckled Holmes.

Looking down at my slightly stained cuff I had to admit he was right, and I laughed in spite of myself.

Holmes and I chatted as we ate, and when I reached for a third sandwich, Holmes smiled and said, "Make certain you leave something for Lestrade."

I refrained from the sandwich and poured Port for the two of us. It was perhaps ten minutes later I heard the bell ring, and a moment after that, I recognized Lestrade's tread on the stairs.

I walked to the door and opened it before he could knock. "Do come in, Lestrade. There are sandwiches on the table and coffee – unless you would care for something a bit stronger."

The inspector entered carrying a small satchel. "I've eaten, Doctor, thank you. Still, a brandy would be greatly appreciated."

I poured him a glass and he settled on the couch. "That was a nice tip about Smith," Lestrade offered. "How did you know he had the jewels, and how on Earth did you figure out where he had hidden them?"

"I would love to tell you everything, Inspector, but just as you protect your sources, so too, must I protect mine."

"I rather figured that was what you might say," replied Lestrade. "I will respect your wishes, but if he hires a skilled barrister, it may be incumbent on you to reveal your sources at trial."

"Well, let's hope it doesn't come to that, Inspector."

"He is a nasty bit of work, Mr. Holmes. He kept insisting that he got the chess set from you. That's why I say it may come up at trial."

At that point I just had to interrupt, "Lestrade, exactly where were the jewels hidden."

"Oh, it was quite a clever hiding place. Mr. Smith had hired someone to hollow out the bottoms of the pieces – both black and white – and then he concealed one jewel in each. The pieces were then packed with clay to prevent the jewels from rolling about and making noise. It also restored some of the weight. The old felt was then re-glued. I assume he was going to smuggle them out of the country at some point."

I looked at my friend but said nothing.

Finally, Holmes replied, "I willingly admit that Smith did acquire the chess set from me, Inspector, but I assure you that I did not conceal the jewels in the pieces. Had I done so, that would make me an accessory of some sort to the robbery at Garrard & Co."

"Well, I've said it more than once myself, and truth be told, so have several other inspectors."

"What's that, Lestrade?" I asked.

"That had he been so inclined, Mr. Holmes would have made a first-rate criminal."

Ignoring Lestrade's remark, Holmes continued, "Smith has committed a great many crimes, Lestrade. However, he is only a middle-man. I would suggest offering him a reduced sentence if he is willing to cooperate. There's no way of telling how high up the ladder he might take you."

"I'll broach that idea to the superintendent, and see if he is inclined to pass it along to the Queen's Counsel."

We chatted a few more minutes, and then Lestrade reached into his satchel. "I almost forgot, but you said you wanted this," and with that he handed a chessboard and the box that had contained the pieces to Holmes, saying, "I don't know why you want these, but here they are. I'll have the pieces returned to you as well after the trial. I must hold them as evidence for now."

"There is no rush, Inspector."

After Lestrade had departed, I looked at Holmes and asked, "How did you do it?"

"Do it? Do what?" he replied innocently. "I pray, Watson, please be a bit more precise with your pronouns."

"You hid those jewels in the chess pieces. I can understand you're bending the law to bring Smith to justice – after all, you've done it before. Still, this really goes beyond the pale."

"Watson, I give you my word, I did no such thing."

"Then how did they get there? More to the point: How did you know where they were – unless you put them there? After all, I was with you when you collected the chess set at Jaques of London."

"Watson, what I am about to tell you must not leave this room. Nor can it makes its way into *The Strand Magazine*. Do we have an understanding?"

I nodded.

"If I had to guess, I should suspect that Mycroft, or someone who works for him concealed the jewels. Remember when I told you that the robbery at Garrard's was an inside job? I was telling the truth. They have the best security in London. For sixteen precious stones, destined for a necklace for Her Majesty, to go missing is inconceivable. Therefore there had to be some degree of cooperation.

"Mycroft was aware of my ongoing battle with Smith and, by extension, with Moriarty. He asked that I bring the chess set, whose purchase he had arranged – or perhaps it was merely a loan – to him at the Diogenes Club. He told me he wanted to examine the pieces. He also instructed me to ask no questions, but that things would work out. He then asked me to leave them with him overnight.

"When I returned the next day, he gave me back the chess set. When I arrived home, I examined the pieces carefully. One of the white rooks in the set I acquired at Jaques had a very faint scratch at its base. Neither of the white rooks in the set Mycroft returned to me had such a mark. I suspected that they had been switched, but suspicions are not proof.

"So I played Smith with the set Mycroft had provided, another of his suggestions. Mycroft also hinted that it would be in my best interests to lose to Smith.

"My brother has since returned the original pieces. They are in my room. Tomorrow, I will place them in the box and return everything to Jaques as though none of this had ever happened."

"But what if you had defeated Smith? What would have happened then?"

"Watson, Smith is a dilettante; he is little more than a gifted amateur. His moves are predictable, and I had to struggle mightily to make those first two games appear as if they had been closely contested. I owe much of that knowledge to Mr. Liu."

"And the third match?"

"Smith is too sharp to think that I would absentmindedly touch a piece, so I had to resort to the coughing fit and the water and then jostling the table. Had I really knocked over the rook, I simply would have said *j'adoube*, which means 'I am adjusting.' However, as you witnessed, Smith was so concerned with winning that any sense of fair play and decorum went out the window. So while I may have suspected what Mycroft was up to, I can say with all honesty, that I did not *know* what he was doing."

I had to marvel at Holmes' logic, even if I suspected that some of it might border on equivocation. However, he brushed away all doubts when he said, "And you will recall that he did kidnap Mrs. Hudson. Some lines, Watson, should never be crossed."

I certainly couldn't argue with that sentiment, but there was one minor point that was nagging at me. "Holmes, I hate to bring this up, but as part of your agreement with Smith, didn't you promise not to live in London if Smith were living here? I mean he is in custody, and I am fairly certain that Scotland Yard is located within the confines of London."

"You make an excellent point, old friend. That is why before Lestrade took him into custody, arrangements were made to house Smith at the relatively new HM Prison Bristol. I wanted him out of London, not so much for the wager, but because I hoped to place him as far as possible from Moriarty's reach, which I know is extensive in London. I am somewhat optimistic that, at least for the moment, since so few people know where Smith has been incarcerated, he will be safe from the Professor and his henchmen.

Chapter 25

Unfortunately, Holmes' optimism was not only misplaced; it was also short-lived. It was but two days later as he and I were just finishing lunch when I heard the front doorbell ring. Seconds after that I heard footfalls as someone rapidly ascended the stairs.

"That sounds as though it could be Lestrade," remarked Holmes. "But I can only recall him taking the steps so quickly on one other occasion."

At that moment, the inspector burst into our sitting room without knocking. I remember thinking, "This must be a matter of some urgency."

"He's gone, Mr. Holmes. He's gone."

"Smith?" inquired my friend. "I thought you had put on extra men. How could he possibly escape?"

"He didn't escape, sir."

"But you said he was 'gone.'"

"And so he is. When the warder went to bring him his breakfast this morning, he found Smith had hanged himself. He had ripped his bedsheet into strips during the night and fashioned a noose which he then ran through the bars in the window."

"Had he told you anything about the Professor?"

"He'd said he was willing to testify, but it was worth his life. Based on your affirmations and with a little encouragement from my superintendent, the Queen's Counsel was working on an arrangement. Smith had said he wouldn't say another word until he had something in writing."

"There is obviously some roguery here. Smith was close to securing, if not his freedom, certainly a greatly reduced sentence. The man had no reason to kill himself."

"We are investigating everyone at the prison who came into contact with Smith, but I must say I don't believe it will lead to much."

"Sad to say, I'm afraid you're correct, and even if you should find out that someone helped facilitate Smith's death, it will only be a minor functionary in the organization. You will never be able to trace it to Moriarty."

"Well, I'll still do my best, Mr. Holmes. I just thought you'd want to know about Smith. If anything else happens, you'll learn of it straightaway."

After Lestrade had left, Holmes lapsed into a sullen silence in his chair. He remained like that for most of the afternoon. He didn't smoke, which I found odd; rather, he just sat there with his fingers steepled under his chin, staring vacantly at the fireplace.

Around five, I heard the front doorbell ring again, and wondered if Lestrade had learned of any new developments. However, I then discerned Mrs. Hudson's footfalls on the stairs. When she knocked at the door, I bade her enter.

She came in carrying a small envelope. "This just arrived for Mr. Holmes by messenger."

Suddenly Holmes snapped out of his brown study and was the very picture of alertness. "I'll take it, dear lady. Thank you very much."

No sooner had she left than Holmes began inspecting the envelope with his glass. "No writing on the front; still, I have seen this same type of envelope on other occasions. Do you recall, Watson?"

"I can't say that I do."

"It's the exact same type of envelope we received following the death of Birdy Edwards."

"You don't mean…"

"I'm afraid I do," said Holmes, cutting me off as he slit the envelope open with his pen knife. He withdrew a single sheet of paper, read it and then handed it to me.

"I have sacrificed a bishop.
I offer a draw, Mr. Holmes."

Holmes merely looked at me and said, "I am inclined to refuse his offer."

Author's notes

The majority of the people and items mentioned in this book are loosely based on real personages and artifacts. Brucastle Abbey is a composite of several of the great country estates of the Victorian era – a number of which still maintain their priest holes today. Among such houses are Harvington Hall and Hindlip Hall, both in Worcestershire, and Naworth Castle in Cumbria.

The history of Simpson's and its association with the game of chess is well-documented. It began life as the Fountain Tavern and was reincarnated as The Great Cigar Divan, which opened in 1828. In 1848, Samuel Reiss joined forces with John Simpson and Simpson's Grand Divan Tavern was born. It eventually became just Simpson's, but now it is part of the Savoy properties and is known as Simpson's-in-the-Strand.

Henry Poole is one of the most respected tailors in London. Among those who have been outfitted by the craftsmen at Poole's are the Emperor Napoleon III, Queen Victoria, and King Edward VII. By the early 1900s, Henry Poole was the largest tailoring establishment of its type in the world, employing 300 tailors and 14 cutters.

Founded in 1735, Garrard & Co. was appointed the first ever official Crown Jewelers in 1843 by Queen Victoria. The firm produced many pieces of silverware and jewelry for the Royal Family, as well as handling the upkeep of the Crown Jewels. The company has dealt with a number of famous jewels, such as the Cullinan I, which is often referred to as "The Great

Star of Africa," and created such pieces as the Imperial Crown of India in 1911, and the Crown of Queen Elizabeth II in 1937. On July 15, 2007, an announcement was made in the "Court Circular" under Buckingham Palace, that the services of Garrard & Co. as crown jeweler were no longer required, with the reason cited being that it was simply "time for a change."

Jaques of London has been making toys and games of various types since 1795. The firm did produce the first series of Staunton chess sets which were signed and numbered by Howard Staunton.

There really was an all-female gang called the Forty Elephants or Forty Thieves. They operated from the late 19th-into the mid-20th century. The members specialised in shoplifting. Operating in the Elephant and Castle section of London, the Forty Thieves were allied with the Elephant and Castle Mob. They would often raid high-end stores in the West End, but they ranged all over the country. The gang was also known to masquerade as housemaids for wealthy families before ransacking their homes. They were known to the police in 1873 and they continued into the 1950s. There are some indications they may have existed since the late 18th century. During the early 20th century the gang was led by Alice Diamond, who was known variously as the Queen of the Forty Thieves and as "Diamond Annie." Morgana is totally my own creation.

In 1889, the Tower Bridge had been under construction for three years. The work had begun on June 21, 1886, and would not conclude for another six years. The bridge was officially opened by Edward, Prince of Wales, and Alexandra, Princess of Wales, on June 30, 1894.

The HMS Bristol Prison, located in Bristol City, Gloucestershire, was relatively new, in 1889, having been opened just six years previously in 1883. The fact that it was far enough away from London made it ideal for my purposes.

Finally, among the villains in the Canon, Culverton Smith, in my humble opinion, ranks third, right behind Professor Moriarty and Charles Augustus Milverton. The temptation to revive him, albeit in the form of a relative, was too tempting to resist.

Acknowledgements

I have always maintained that writing, at least as I practice it, is a lonely task. I tend to write late at night when everyone is in bed and the house is still. However, it has been made somewhat less onerous by the encouragement and patience of friends and family, especially my wife, who have supported and cheered me on in my endeavors.

I should be terribly remiss if I failed to thank my publisher, Steve Emecz, who makes the process painless; and the enormously talented Brian Belanger, whose skill as a cover designer is unmatched.

No book is complete without a solid line edit, and Deborah Annakin Peters continues to provide that as well as a number of invaluable suggestions that improve all of my books immeasurably. She also makes certain that my Britishisms are correct and that no Americanisms creep in. My works are so much better because of her diligence and care.

I also owe a considerable debt to Robert Katz, a good friend, who remains the finest Sherlockian I know. He has continued to encourage me and is kind enough to read my efforts with an eye toward accuracy – both with regard to the Canon, and perhaps more importantly, to common sense.

To Francine and Richard Kitts, two outstanding Sherlockians, for their unflagging support and encouragement.

To my brother, Edward, and my sister, Arlene, who continue to believe in me even when I am doubting myself.

To all my former students who have read and enjoyed my books and offered kind words of encouragement.

Finally, to all those, and there are far too many to name, whose support for my earlier efforts has made me see just what a wonderful life I have and what great people I am surrounded by. So to all those who have read my earlier works, a sincere thank you.

To say that I am in the debt of all those mentioned here doesn't even begin to scratch the surface of my gratitude.

Finally, if there are errors in this book – and I'm pretty sure there are – the only person responsible for them is me.

About the author

Richard T. Ryan is a native New Yorker, having been born and raised on Staten Island. He majored in English at St. Peter's College in Jersey City and pursued his graduate studies, concentrating on medieval literature, at the University of Notre Dame in Indiana.

After teaching high school and college for more than a decade, he joined the staff of the Staten Island Advance newspaper. He worked there for nearly 30 years, rising through the ranks to become news editor. When he retired in 2016, he held the position of publications manager for that paper although he still prefers the title, news editor.

In addition to his first novel, "The Vatican Cameos: A Sherlock Holmes Adventure," he has written "The Stone of Destiny: A Sherlock Holmes Adventure," "The Druid of Death" "The Merchant of Menace," "Through a Glass Starkly" and "Three May Keep a Secret." He is also the author of "B Is for Baker Street: My First Sherlock Holmes Book," which he wrote for his grandchildren, Riley and Henry. He has also penned three trivia books, including "The Official Sherlock Holmes Trivia Book."

In a different medium, he can also boast at having "Deadly Relations," a mystery-thriller produced off-Broadway on two separate occasions.

And if that weren't enough, he is also the very proud father of two children, Dr. Kaitlin Ryan-Smith and Michael

Ryan, and the incredibly proud grandfather of the aforementioned Riley Grace and Henry Robert.

He has been married for more than 40 years to his wife, Grace, and continues to marvel at her incredible patience in putting up with him and his computer illiteracy.

He is currently at work on his eighth novel, a period piece set in the Middle Ages, which just keeps getting put off by Holmes stories. After finishing that, if he ever does, he plans to take another look into the box he purchased at auction and see what tales remain.

Keep reading:

For a sneak peek at Richard Ryan's latest novel,
tentatively titled,

The Devil's Disciples:

A Sherlock Holmes Adventure

The Devil's Disciples:

A Sherlock Holmes Adventure

by Richard T. Ryan

Chapter 1 – December 14, 1884

It was a rarity when I arose before Sherlock Holmes, but I had been summoned to my surgery quite early that day due to a medical emergency. I returned home and was finishing my breakfast just as Holmes emerged from his bedroom. Enraged by what I had just read in *The Times*, I exclaimed, "Holmes, they've done it again!"

My friend looked at me in bewilderment and said calmly, "Pray be precise with your pronouns, Watson. Having not yet had the opportunity to peruse the papers, I am totally at sea with regard to whom your 'they' might refer, nor would I care to hazard a guess as to exactly what 'they' have done as the 'it' in your sentence is also singularly uninformative."

"The Fenians! The Fenians!" I yelled. "They tried to bomb London Bridge last evening."

"It would seem apparent from your use of the word 'tried' that the attempt was unsuccessful," he offered.

It was the morning of December 14, 1884, and we were now in the third year of a campaign that had seen the Irish Republican Brotherhood, in conjunction with its American counterpart, a group called the *Clan na Gael*, employing bombs as their weapons of choice in a series of attacks that had shown little, if any, discrimination. "That makes at least a dozen attempted bombings in the last three years."

"I believe the exact number is fourteen attempts – although there may be others of which I am unaware – involving some twenty bombs," asserted Holmes. "Fortunately, on at least three occasions the bombs were either discovered before they could explode and they were successfully defused, or the timing device malfunctioned in some way thus preventing the bomb's detonation. Now do tell me more about this latest bombing at the bridge."

"According to the *Times,* members of the Irish Republican Brotherhood or sympathisers with their cause were attempting to plant a bomb at one of the piers under the bridge when it exploded prematurely. Surprisingly, little damage appears to have been done to the bridge, but windows on both sides of the Thames were blown out, and the bombers' boat was completely destroyed. As a result, the police are uncertain if the men, somehow managed to escape or if they fell victim to the explosion."

"I should think given the severity of the blast that any would-be bombers perished as a result. Still, I suppose we shall have to wait until the bodies are recovered – if indeed, they ever are."

As you might expect, the latest atrocity perpetrated by the Fenians was all anyone could talk about for the next few days. Whether at my surgery or at my club, the bombing was on everyone's mind. Judging from the snatches of conversation I picked up from people I passed in the street, Londoners were starting to feel unsafe in their own city. More concerning was the fact that I thought I detected a certain unease regarding, and perhaps a growing mistrust of the government.

Things grew even worse a week later, when on December 20, the *Illustrated London News* ran a full-page drawing on its front depicting the flash of the explosion under the bridge as seen by witnesses crossing over the span above. It was a remarkable drawing, but all it did was rub anew the already raw nerves of the average Londoner.

The holidays were marred to a degree when news spread on Christmas Day that the mutilated remains of one of the bombers had been discovered downriver. Although the body of the other man was never recovered, the police were later able to identify the dead men as two Americans, William Mackey Lomasney and John Fleming.

The bombers were eventually identified because a landlord reported to police that dynamite had been found in the rooms he had rented to two American gentlemen who had gone missing after 13 December.

With that bit of information, the police were able to piece together who had been behind the attack. As it turned out, both men had already been under surveillance by the police, both in America and in Britain. There was some speculation a third man might have been involved, but the authorities were never able to say with absolute certainty whether the bombers numbered two or three.

Although 1895 arrived with hope and fanfare, things quickly turned somber when a bomb exploded in the Gower Train Station on January 2. Fortunately, no one was hurt or injured, but the capital was on edge once again.

One evening, a few days after the latest atrocity, I asked Holmes why he had not taken more of an interest in the case. He looked at me and then replied rather cryptically, "What makes you think I haven't?"

I debated pursuing the issue and then decided against it. Holmes and I had been friends for only a few years, and though I had assisted on a number of cases, we were still trying to ascertain exactly where we stood with each other. I also knew that if Holmes wanted to make me privy to his actions, he would – but only when he was ready.

As you might expect, after a week or so, the train station bombing like the others before it, was replaced with the latest scandal at home and news from abroad. By mid-January, the 17th to be exact, spirits were buoyed when the British scored a resounding victory at the Battle of Abu Klea in the long-running Mahdist War.

However, our joy was short-lived because on 20 January another bomb exploded on a Metropolitan train at Gower Street. There were no fatalities although several passengers suffered minor cuts from broken glass. And then just as things were beginning to calm down after that, on 24 January, three bombs exploded in the House of Commons chamber, in the banqueting room in the Tower of London, and in Westminster Hall.

I felt certain that Holmes would now involve himself in the affair, and I was proven correct when the next morning the bell sounded at around nine o'clock. Mrs. Hudson knocked on the door a moment later. Holmes bade her enter and when she did it was apparent that she was quite flustered.

"Mr. Holmes," she began, "there's a gentleman downstairs asking if he might have a few moments of your time." With that she handed Holmes the man's card. My friend glanced at it and said, "By all means, show him up."

Since Holmes often required privacy when interviewing clients, I rose and started to go to my bedroom. "Stay, Watson," said Holmes, "I think you may want to hear what our visitor has to say. You never know, it may make a fitting subject for one of those tales with which you have been busying yourself of late."

A few minutes later, a dapper young man of perhaps 30, entered our rooms. He bowed at Holmes and then me, and said, "Mr. Holmes, I am Jeremy Brownson, first deputy to Assistant Commissioner James Monro."

"Both of your names are well-known to me," replied Holmes.

Brownson looked at Holmes and then continued, "I do not normally take such liberties as dropping in on someone unannounced, but the situation confronting us is one of such urgency that I am quite willing to forego social niceties if it means we arrive at a resolution sooner rather than later."

"Pray be seated," said Holmes. "Would you care for coffee or tea?"

"Nothing for me," replied Brownson.

"You have come about the Fenian bombings?" inquired Holmes.

Our guest looked first at Holmes and then me and then he returned his gaze to Holmes as he sat there in silence.

"You may speak freely in front of Dr. Watson," said Holmes. "He is the epitome of discretion."

I was quite moved by the compliment my friend had just paid me, but I said nothing.

Our guest looked at me and said, "I trust you understand everything I am about to tell you must remain in the strictest confidence. Lives will depend on *your* sense of 'discretion.'"

I nodded and said, "I understand, Mr. Brownson,"

Our visitor then began to recount the numerous outrages perpetrated by various members of the Irish Republican Brotherhood working in concert with members of *Clan na Gael* over the last three years. I watched Holmes carefully, and I could see that on one or two occasions he was surprised at what he was being told.

After about fifteen minutes, our visitor concluded, "Thus far, we have been most fortunate. Between our spies in the Brotherhood, informers, and sheer ineptitude on the part of the bombers, the damage has been largely confined to property. While many people have been injured – some quite seriously – there have been only three deaths to date."

"Yes, the young boy who perished in January 1881 when the barracks at Salford in Lancashire were targeted, and I presume the other two fatalities would be the Americans who attempted to blow up the London Bridge."

"You have it exactly, Mr. Holmes. I can see that you have given this some thought."

"Indeed, I have," replied my friend. "Had you not called here today, you might have seen me in the offices of Assistant Commissioner Monro tomorrow where I would have offered my services."

"And trust me, sir, he would have accepted your offer."

"So, what's to be done?"

"As you can see Mr. Holmes, the bombers grow bolder. You may recall last May bombs exploded at the headquarters of Metropolitan Police Criminal Investigation Department and the Special Irish Branch in Scotland Yard; in the basement of the Carlton Club, a well-known haunt for Conservative MPs; and outside the home of Conservative MP Sir Watkin Williams Wynn."

"I recall it all too well," replied Holmes. "Ten people were injured and I believe a fourth bomb, planted at the foot of Nelson's Column, failed to explode."

"You knew about the fourth bomb? But how? We kept that under wraps so as not to frighten the citizenry any more than necessary."

"I have my methods," replied Holmes.

"And did you know about the bombs on the ships as well?"

"I assume you are referring to the disguised explosives discovered back in 1881 aboard the SS Malta and the SS Bavaria which were berthed in Liverpool."

"Again, you hit the mark."

"I have taken a special interest in these bombings for reasons of my own, but I place my powers, such as they may be, at your disposal."

"As I've said, Mr. Holmes, we have spies in their ranks, but their knowledge is limited to their immediate circle. This is a group that has roots on both sides of the Atlantic. Making matters worse, there are sections of Ireland where they are seemingly beyond the reach of the law – unless they slip up badly.

"Add to that the vagaries of the government where Mr. Gascoyne-Cecil and Mr. Disraeli seem to be playing a game of musical chairs with the position of Prime Minister and any political solution to the problem will not soon be forthcoming."

"What is it you would like me to do?" asked Holmes.

"Somehow, you must find a way to end this reign of terror. Tensions between native Englishmen and the Irish who emigrated here after the potato famine have always been strained, but these senseless bombings have brought things to a boil. Anyone who speaks with even a hint of a brogue is looked upon with suspicion, and heaven help the poor Irishman walking through the streets carrying a bag."

"I will certainly give the matter some thought," replied Holmes. "Hopefully, I will be able to devise a plan to capture the dynamiters so that people may sleep in their beds without fear of their neighbors and what the next day may bring."

"It is imperative that you do so, Mr. Holmes. One of the men we have inserted into the group has alerted us to the fact that they now have a new, and if he is to be believed, far more proficient bomb-maker."

"That was to be expected," said Holmes, "as these groups evolve, they also advance in terms of the methods they employ."

"That's true, Mr. Holmes. However, he has also informed us that they plan to step-up the campaign by detonating multiple bombs on a daily basis until Ireland is given its freedom."

CPSIA information can be obtained
at www.ICGtesting.com
Printed in the USA
BVHW070329161222
654335BV00012B/758

9 781804 240854